KT-179-877

9030 00004 8864 9

Gun Barrel Justice

Jason Connor, a wandering preacher, stumbles across a wagon and its dead occupants. He decides he must deliver the only survivor, a young boy, to his aunt and uncle. But before he can do so, he must shoot his way through the gang responsible for the murders.

The trouble is not over yet. When he comes upon the scene of a double lynching, the discovery puts Connor on a collision course with the executioners. The killers keep coming and the gun barrels grow hot as assassins stake a claim for the bounty on his head. The Bible-spouting gunman deals out gun barrel justice as he sends killer after killer to Hell.

By the same author

Zacchaeus Wolfe
Massacre at Empire Fastness
Hammer of God
Paths of Death
Caleb Blood
Wild Justice
Maclean
Hornstone

Writing as Elliot James

Hot Spur
Son of a Gun
Hal Grant's War

Writing as Gary Astill

Texas Rendezvous

Writing as Henry Christopher

Vengeance Unbound

Writing as Jim Wilson

Carson's Revenge

Gun Barrel Justice

P. McCormac

A Black Horse Western

ROBERT HALE · LONDON

© P. McCormac 2016
First published in Great Britain 2016

ISBN 978-0-7198-1807-3

Robert Hale Limited
Clerkenwell House
Clerkenwell Green
London EC1R 0HT

www.halebooks.com

The right of P. McCormac to be identified as
author of this work has been asserted by him
in accordance with the Copyright, Designs and
Patents Act 1988

LONDON BOROUGH OF WANDSWORTH	
9030 00004 8864 9	
Askews & Holts	04-Feb-2016
AF WES	£14.50
	WW15019344

Printed and bound in Great Britain by
CPI Antony Rowe, Chippenham and Eastbourne

CHAPTER ONE

Jason Connor eased up his sorrel and examined the scene before him. A wagon was set on the trail with debris scattered around it. He sat for some minutes figuring out what had happened. He was guessing it was no accident – or why would the wagon have been emptied and the contents scattered about?

He let his eye wander over the surrounding hills. Nothing moved within his range of vision. As far as he could make out there was no sign of life either in the vicinity of the wagon or anywhere nearby. Whoever or whatever the cause of the upheaval had moved on. He undid the loop securing his Peacemaker, eased the weapon in the holster and nudged his horse forward. As he approached the abandoned vehicle he never let up his vigilance – scanning the area around the wagon as well as watching for movement in the nearby countryside.

Clothing, cooking utensils and items of food were scattered about in a wide untidy arc. There was a sudden movement and immediately Connor's gun was in his hand. He grimaced ruefully as a couple of vultures lifted off. He had not been aware of the scavengers until his approach had disturbed them.

'Hell cursed creatures,' he muttered as he replaced his gun. 'At least it shows there ain't anyone left alive.'

He surveyed the scene, noting the items strewn around.

There wasn't much of any value left amongst the debris. He dismounted and walked to the far side of the stranded vehicle. It was then he saw the bodies sprawled in the dirt – a man and a woman both with gunshot wounds. Connor tipped his hat back and pulled out the makings.

'Shot from the front. No sign of any weapons. I guess it was robbery. Poor souls. I wonder where they were heading.'

He finished rolling his cigarette and lit up, blowing a long plume of smoke in the direction of the two bodies.

'Well,' he signed, 'ain't nothing for it. I guess I'll have to bury these poor souls. Help send them on their last journey.'

Connor found a shovel tied to the side of the wagon and, slinging it over his shoulder, stepped off the road and walked a few paces towards a growth of cactus. It was then he saw the boot. Its small size made him think immediately of a child or female.

'By the good Lord above, but this is a dastardly affair. I sure hope there are no more bodies lying around.'

He stepped towards the cactus and the boot moved. Almost as he saw it twitch Connor again made that bewildering swift movement and his gun appeared once more in his hand.

'Come out, whoever you are. Come out with your hands plainly in sight. I won't shoot unless you give me cause but I have a gun here primed and ready. I don't want no trouble. It looks to me as if there has been more than enough grief here today and I don't want to add to that.'

The boot moved and a young boy shuffled into sight. His clothes were dusty and his face smudged from what Connor guessed was tears. He immediately holstered his gun.

'Son, my name is Jason Connor. I don't mean you no harm. I take it you were travelling with the folks on that wagon out on the road there?'

The boy nodded, raised a hand and wiped it across his eyes.

'I ain't crying, sir,' he said.

'Sure, I know that. There are folk lying out there on the road. I take it they're kin of yours?'

'Ma and Pa and Sis. I guess they're dead.'

Connor's eyes narrowed. He dug the shovel into the dirt and squatted down and pulled on his smoke. He had seen only two bodies and they were both adults.

'Your pa and your ma and your sis – how old is sis?'

'Twelve.'

'I see, and how old are you?'

'Ten, sir.'

'Your folks sure taught you good manners, son. What's your name?'

'Alexander Leopold Amery, sir.'

'Well, Alexander Leopold Amery, there is no sign of your sister out there. Do you know what happened to her?'

'They took her with them. I heard her weeping. I couldn't do nothing.'

'Son, nobody could do anything against armed bandits. Don't feel bad about it. Are you hungry?'

'I don't think so, sir.'

'Alexander, you can call me Jason.'

He stood and picked up the shovel.

'I was about to bury your family but we can get you something to eat afore I perform that duty.'

'No sir, I'll help you dig the grave.'

'I'd appreciate your help but you don't have to. You might want to sit quietly somewhere while I do it.'

'No, sir, I want to help you. I helped Pa on the farm when I wasn't in school. Times he said he couldn't manage without me.'

There was a catch in the boy's voice as he spoke. Connor smiled reassuringly at the boy.

'You are very brave, Alexander. I was nowhere near as brave as you when I was your age. Let's get started, then. Soonest begun, soonest mended, as my old horse is fond of telling me. Here, you take this shovel while I go and see if I can liberate a pick.'

The soil was rocky and difficult to dig but after some effort they dug a hole a yard or so deep and wide enough to take the two bodies.

'You wait here while I fetch your ma and pa and we will lay them to rest.'

Connor ferried the bodies to the grave and carefully arranged them side by side. Folding the arms so they rested over the torso, he walked back to his horse and rummaged about in his saddlebags. When he returned he was wearing a dog collar and carrying a Bible.

'Are you a preacher, sir?'

'I suppose one might say that, though my church has disowned me. Like Lucifer I was banished from the community of God – "excommunicated" is the word they use. But I still try to carry on the Lord's work. So if you have no objection I'll perform the ritual for the dead and send these good souls on their last journey?'

Connor cleared his throat and nodded solemnly to the boy.

'Let us pray, I am the Resurrection and the life, saith the Lord; he that believeth in me, though he were dead, yet shall he live; and whosoever liveth and believeth in me shall never die....'

The young boy stood quietly as the man prayed over his dead parents. At one point a sob broke from him. Finally, Connor took out a small flask and sprinkled water over the corpses.

'In sure and certain hope of the Resurrection of eternal life,' he intoned, 'we commend to Almighty God the souls of our brother and sister and we commit their bodies to the ground – ashes to ashes, dust to dust. The Lord bless them and keep them; the Lord make his face shine upon them and be gracious unto them and give them peace. Amen.

'Now Alexander if you would fetch a blanket we will cover up your parents. I want you to understand these are but vessels of clay. The souls of your parents are right now partying up in Paradise with Jesus and all his saints. They're looking down on us now and thanking us for performing these rites for them.'

When the grave was filled in the preacher hacked a couple of branches and fashioned a simple cross which he rammed into the grave mound.

'We will sing a psalm now and then we will have done our Christian duty.'

Connor lifted his voice and began to sing.

I will lift up mine eyes unto the hills;
from whence cometh my help?
My help cometh even from the Lord,
who hath made heaven and earth.

He had a fine tenor voice and his singing strangely moved the young boy. At last Connor closed his Bible.

'Alexander, we shall have a bite to eat and then we shall go and seek out the sinners that have committed these foul deeds.'

CHAPTER TWO

Leaving the boy to sort through the scattered contents of the wagon for his belongings, Connor got a fire going. He fried bacon and beans and sliced up bread.

'Find yourself a plate and a mug among that lot and come and get some grub down you,' he called.

'I ain't hungry.'

'Just bring a plate like I told you. In my experience boys are always hungry.'

Alexander squatted by the fire staring into the flames. Connor heaped beans and bacon and bread on the plate, saying a short prayer over the food. He held the plate out but the boy ignored it.

'Are you an ungrateful kind of person?' he asked.

'No, sir.'

'I went to the bother to cook this here food and now you won't eat it.'

'I don't mean to be disrespectful, sir.'

'I know that, Alexander. Just you do me a favour and eat a little. A growing boy like you needs good grub in him.'

The youngster obediently took the loaded plate.

'I don't know if you drink coffee. It's all I got unless you prefer water.'

'I'll have water, thank you, sir.'

Connor finished eating, poured another coffee and rolled a cigarette.

'I guess you're too young to smoke and I sure wouldn't recommend it. I got hooked myself when I was even younger than you.'

Connor noted the food was disappearing fast from the boy's plate. He hacked another slice of bread and handed it across.

'Thank you, sir.'

'You can call me Jason. It would be a mite easier on the ear than all this "sir" business.'

'Yes, sir ... Jason, sir,' the boy said through a mouthful of bread.

'Maybe you could tell me what happened here. Though it is easy enough to read the signs. If you don't feel like talking that's all right.'

'It was my fault. I needed a pee and I asked Pa to stop so I could go. I was behind a tree when I heard the shooting and when I looked there were men gathered round the wagon shooting and Pa had his gun but they shot him anyway and Ma took up the gun and they shot her, too. I was afraid and I didn't come to help. I just hid and now they're all dead because of me....'

His voice trailed off and the tears spilled from his eyes and then he was sobbing and saying something, though the words were lost amidst his weeping. The big man moved over beside the boy and put a comforting hand on his shoulder.

'There, there. Y'know, it seems to me it weren't your fault. Those fellas would have shot your folk anyhow even if they hadn't stopped to let you off. They were evil men. You were spared so you could bear witness against them. You and I, we will bring them to justice. Can you recall how many there were?'

'I counted five.'

'Would you know them again when we come across them?'

'Yes, sir – I mean Jason, sir.'

'OK, Alexander, if you've finished eating we'd better get started. I fear for your sister's safety.'

It was late afternoon when Connor spotted the buzzards. He said nothing but noted their position and guessed they would pass close to whatever it was that was attracting them. When they drew nearer he pulled up his horse.

'Alexander, I want you to climb down here. I need to go off the trail a mite. I won't be long.'

The boy turned scared eyes to his companion.

'Are you going to leave me here?'

'No, I am not leaving you. I'll look after you till we get you somewhere safe. So rest assured on that. I just got to see to something over yonder.'

He pointed vaguely in the direction of the buzzards. The birds could be seen rising up and swooping down again as if they were squabbling over something on the ground. He had a notion he knew what it was and did not want the boy along in case his suspicions were correct. Gently but firmly he deposited the youngster on the ground.

'Sit by that rock over there. I won't be but a short time.'

He had a sudden thought.

'Can you read?'

'Yes, sir, Mister Jason. Ma taught me my letters.'

The youngster was staring up at him with that scared look in his eyes. Connor smiled reassuringly and reached into his saddlebag and produced his Bible.

'Here, you read this while I'm gone. That'll show you I ain't going to abandon you. I would never normally part with my Bible. You should feel very privileged that I am lending this to you. Ain't everyone I would trust with this book. But I know you are trustworthy, Alexander. So you sit over there on that rock and read. When I come back I'll want you to tell me what you read.'

Alexander solemnly took the Bible.

'You take good care of that book now. That Bible has travelled many a mile with me and is a comfort to me on my journey through this vale of tears.'

The boy watched Connor till he was out of sight, then settled on the rock and opened the Bible.

Connor threaded his way through the maze of rocks and bushes towards the carrion birds. When he was near enough for them to be aware of his approach some raised their heads to stare in his direction. They were feeding on something bloody and he could not make out what it was. His horse did not like the smell and he had to keep urging it to move forward. The birds were looking in his direction and warning him away with their angry hissing, and this too was spooking his horse. And then Connor groaned as he realized his worst fears had come true.

'Oh, dear Lord above, I reckon we found Alexander's unfortunate sister.'

CHAPTER THREE

Connor stood over the body with his head bowed deep in prayer. He took his slicker from where it was fastened to the rear of his saddle and, with great tenderness, rolled the mutilated body in the garment, noting that some of the wounds had not been made solely by the depredations of the feeding buzzards.

'Dear child, I reckon those human vultures violated the sanctity of your innocent young body afore dumping you here. I just hope you didn't suffer too much but I fear that hope is one in which I do not put much faith. The misdeeds of those evil men are mounting and the penalty will be severe.'

The horse whickered in protest when he slung the bundle

across the saddle.

'I know Zipporah, old gal. I like it even less than you to have to transport the body of an innocent female back to her brother. How am I going to break the news to him without breaking his heart. I fear it is breaking my heart, also. I sorely grieve for this family so brutally destroyed by evil men.'

Alexander stood up as Connor approached leading the horse with its grisly burden.

'I have grave news for you, Alexander.'

'It's Gertrude, ain't it?'

'I'm afraid so. I am truly sorry.'

'Can I see her?'

'The buzzards were at her. She was dead afore they would have begun. I don't suppose she suffered.'

He told the lie knowing from the damaged body the child had suffered brutal abuse at the hands of her captors.

'We have the sorry task of laying your sister to rest.'

Connor performed the last rites for the daughter of the man and woman he had buried earlier that same day, attended by the one remaining member of the family. They piled rocks upon the grave and once more he made a crude cross to mark the place.

'Now we have done our duty by your sister we best be moving on,' Connor told his young charge.

Alexander turned solemn eyes to Connor.

'Will you lend me your gun?'

For long moments Connor looked at the boy, his young determined face pale and set.

'For what would you be wanting a gun?' Connor asked, though he guessed what was on the boy's mind.

'I want to kill the men that murdered my family.'

'Let's get going. We'll have to make camp soon, for night is almost upon us. We will talk about this matter over supper.'

They were riding for some time when they came across a stream and Connor noted the tracks where riders had stopped to water their horses. He did not let on to Alexander he was following the trail of the gang who had so brutally wiped out his family.

'This looks a likely spot to camp,' he said. 'While I get supper going I want you to have a good wash. Cleanliness is next to Godliness, as is said.'

He handed the boy a piece of soap.

'Don't lose the soap. I'll need it in the morning.'

Alexander wandered down stream and within sight of the man began his ablutions. Connor in the meantime got a fire going and poured beans into a pan of water. When the mix was simmering he added an onion along with some chillies and strips of dried beef. Deep in thought he sat by the fire and stared at the flames. By the time the boy returned the stew was almost ready and Connor had a pot of coffee bubbling on the fire. Connor divided up the stew and handed Alexander a plate and a spoon.

'There you are, son. Do you want to say grace?'

'No, I don't see any point in praying to someone as cruel as God.'

'I can see you are angry, Alexander, but it ain't God as committed those evil deeds. God gives us free will to do good or evil. That was the lesson in the Garden of Eden. He told Adam and Eve not to eat the fruit of the tree of good and evil, but they chose to ignore his warning. That one small act of disobedience let loose all the wickedness we see in the world today.'

'Will you lend me your gun?'

'Let's eat and then we'll talk about that.

Connor bowed his head over his plate.

'Thank you Lord for the fare we partake of tonight

15

through your benevolence.'

They ate in silence until Connor eventually spoke again.

'I guess you have revenge on your mind. You want to catch up on those killers and shoot it out with them.'

'Yes, I do.'

'There are five of them, as you told me when we first met. Five very brutal and dangerous men. Killers all. Any one of which would gun you down with about as much thought as they would give to swatting a fly. Now don't take me wrong; I ain't belittling you none. If you were a grown man you would still have trouble tackling that gang. I wouldn't want to be responsible for assisting you in committing suicide by handing you a gun so as you could go against a gang of killers.'

'I ain't afraid.'

'No, you don't strike me as being the timorous type. I've watched you today and through the dreadful things that happened you stayed strong. You'd be a good fella to ride the trail with.'

'Does that mean you ain't going to help me?'

'I didn't say that. I'm just pointing out the impracticalities of giving you a gun to allow you to go after those murderers. I feel I would be giving you a death sentence if I did. I don't think I could live with that.'

'I can use a gun. Pa and me went hunting. I was a good shot. Could hit turkeys on the wing.'

'My, my, Alexander, I am impressed. Like I say you'd be a good man to ride the trail with. Have you got any relations you could go to, I mean as would take you in?'

'My Aunt Ellen and Uncle Sidney. We were on our way to join them. Uncle Sidney wrote telling Pa there was good land to be had in Oregon. So Pa sold his farm and we were....'

Alexander's voice broke and the tears came.

Connor rolled a smoke and poured another mug of coffee. He stretched back against his saddle and sighed deeply. For a long time he stayed like that thinking over his options.

'Tell you what, Alexander; I ain't got a lot going at the moment. If you like I could take you to Oregon.'

There was no reply and he looked over. Alexander was slumped on the ground fast asleep. Connor made up the blankets and rolled the boy into them. While he did this the boy remained fast asleep.

'I guess you're plumb worn out, little fella. Losing all your family in one day is a mighty hard thing to handle.'

In the morning Connor told Alexander of his decision to deliver him to his aunt and uncle.

'I know you can look after yourself and could get to Oregon on your own but I like your company and it would make my wanderings less lonesome.'

'Have you thought any more about lending me your gun? I could buy it off you. I know I ain't got any money but I could borrow from my uncle and pay you.'

'Son, it frets my heart to see you're still set on this vengeance trail. It's a terrible thing to kill a man. Life is his most precious possession. When you fire that gun and that fella drops to the dirt it makes a man stop short and think of his own mortality.'

'Have you ever killed anyone?'

Connor stayed still for a moment before answering.

'To my great regret I have indeed taken life. It weighs heavy on me and not a day passes that I don't pray for the souls of those who have perished at my hand.'

'You said souls. How many were there?'

'Time for us to be moving on, Alexander.'

They had been travelling most of the day when they sighted the town. Connor took out his dog collar and to all intents and purposes when he rode into the township of Moore he was just a shabby preacher with a young boy perched alongside him.

The doubly burdened horse cantered along the rutted road past the town boundary and past the neatly tended gardens with painted picket fences and houses with porches and verandas well maintained. They progressed through the outskirts coming to the main business sector. Connor pulled up at the sheriff's office.

'We better report what happened. Wait here.'

There was no one in the office and when Connor came out again Alexander had dismounted and was standing across the road and fussing a mare tied to the hitching rail outside a saloon among a row of other horses. Connor opened his saddlebag and removed a buckskin wrapped bundle. From this he extracted a gun and holster which he clipped to his belt and tugged his coat to cover it. He loosened his Peacemaker and strode across the street.

'Alexander, what is it?'

The boy turned tearful eyes to him.

'It's Chessboard. He was our horse.'

'You sure?'

Alexander pointed to the markings on the mare's chest. They did indeed bear a slight resemblance to the pattern of a chequer board.

'OK, son. I want you to go back across the road and stay with my horse. If anything happens to me you ride out of here and carry on to Oregon.'

'What are you going to do?'

'I'll go in there and find out who it was that brought Chessboard here.'

CHAPTER FOUR

The saloon was called The Doe and the Dragon. Connor walked inside and stood for a moment scrutinizing the inhabitants. He spotted the big man with the badge standing at the bar with three other drinkers. For a few moments he stood just inside, then walked across to the lawman. The men ignored him.

'Sheriff, I want to report a crime.'

The beefy face turned towards Connor – eyes examined him, noting the dog collar.

'Howdy, Reverend. I'm drinking at the moment. The law office is closed for now. You'll have to come back in the morning.'

One of the men with the sheriff sniggered.

'What happened, Reverend – someone break into the poor box?'

That remark brought a few guffaws.

'I can't wait till the morning, Sheriff. I'm interested in a horse tied to the rail outside and want to know the fella that claims to own it.'

'What horse is that?'

'A mare with a particular marking on its chest like a chessboard.'

The men shifted about, the amusement fading as they examined the newcomer.

'What about that horse, mister?'

'That horse belonged to a young family on their way to Oregon.'

'What you trying to say, preacher?'

The speaker was dark-bearded, his skin swarthy where his beard did not cover.

'I'm asking who owns that horse. Just a simple question. No need to get all jumpy about it. I'm sure there's a logical explanation for that horse being here.'

'Git the hell out of here afore someone throws you out. Preacher or no preacher, you ain't got no call coming in here asking questions about things that don't concern you. So go on – git.'

'You see that horse does concern me,' Connor said mildly. 'I buried the family who owned that horse. Someone ambushed and killed the people in that wagon. They abducted a young girl also and, after abusing her, left her for the buzzards. I buried her also. So you see I want to talk to the man who brought that horse here. He might be able to tell me something that may point me towards the villains that were responsible for the deaths of that innocent young family.'

'That horse was bought fair and square. No one here knows anything about no family or no killings. We've been here all week so don't go making assumptions where there are none.'

'Strange you should mention the timeframe for this crime. I did not say when the killings took place. But if the horse was purchased legit, then you'll have a bill of sale?'

'What the hell you talking about? The fella as I bought it from was in a hurry and lit out afore I could think to get a bill from him.'

'In that case you bought a stolen horse. I came in here to report the crime to the sheriff.'

The bearded man took a step forward.

'I told you once to git. I ain't telling you again. Now git afore I lay the barrel of my gun across that thick skull of yours and throw you out.'

'Sheriff, this man is threatening violence against me. As

a law-abiding citizen I demand you arrest this fella or at least caution him regarding his offensive behaviour.'

The sheriff smirked across at Connor.

'Reverend, this man is a friend of mine. You come in my town making false accusations against people, you deserve all the abuse that might be ladled out. So take the man's advice and leave. Leave the saloon, leave the town, and leave us in peace to get on with our drinking.'

'I guess there is no justice to be had in a town where the law lies down with the criminals. I shall leave, gentlemen but in time there must be a reckoning for such evil deeds.'

'Hang on, Reverend – are you calling my friends criminals?'

'Each of us must know the evil in one's heart. You are testifying that these men have been here in the past few days and never left the town, yet I never mentioned when the crime was committed?'

'Hell, I've had enough of this holy man.'

The bearded man reached out a hand and pushed Connor, then yelled in pain as the preacher gripped his hand and twisted savagely. The man knelt down before Connor, his mouth open in moaning agony.

'Now you are on your knees, sinner, we can perhaps pray together for your redemption.'

With his other hand the man on the floor reached for his gun. Connor stepped back and kicked him in the face, throwing him back among his companions. The sheriff swore and blundered forward towards Connor.

'Son of a bitch,' he growled, 'I'm arresting you.'

The sheriff stopped abruptly, staring down at the gun that had appeared in the preacher's hand.

'I don't think so, Sheriff. I have a suspicion the fella on the floor there is a murderer and if you will allow me to take him outside I have a witness that can prove his guilt or innocence. If he is indeed not guilty of the crimes I will apologize and make reparation by praying for your salvation. I get the uneasy feeling you are all trying too hard to cover up something.'

'What the hell kind of preacher are you – pulling a gun on a fella? That ain't very Christian-like.'

'You think not, Sheriff? The Lord tells us to condemn the sinner and bring all wrongdoers to justice. I am but an instrument of the Lord. Now if you will all step back and let me escort this fella outside, this can be resolved quite amicably.'

The bearded man was on his feet by now and staring sullenly at the preacher.

'You won't get away with this, Preacher. You don't know who you are messing with. My name is Victor Harris and these men are my brothers. You picked the wrong people to tangle with.'

'It's them, Jason!'

The shrill voice came from behind and Connor realized Alexander must have wandered in from the street.

'Stay back!' he called and then there came the sound of a struggle.

'Let me go,' Alexander yelled.

The men Connor was holding at bay were looking beyond him.

'Preacher, we got your boy. Put up your gun and no harm will come to him.'

Connor risked a glance over his shoulder. Alexander was struggling in the grip of a man who had a gun in one hand and his other hand was twisted in the boy's shirt.

'Looks like we hold all the aces, Preacher. You going to give up quietly, or do we have to hurt the boy?'

There came the sound of a slap and Alexander cried out.

'All right, looks like we got stalemate. I'll back off and we'll leave quietly.'

There was a shot and Connor instinctively ducked.

'Not so fast, Preacher! You drop that gun or the boy will die. It won't take much to blow his head off.'

'Don't harm him. He's only a kid. He's suffered much over the last few days.'

'It's your call, fella. Drop your weapon and this can all end peaceably.'

'You promise to let the boy go and we ride out of town.'

'Mister,' the sheriff butted in, 'the sooner you're out of here the better for everyone. So why don't you do as you're told and get the Hell out of here?'

Connor holstered his gun and backed away warily watching his adversaries. The man holding Alexander shoved him roughly to one side.

'Time to die, Preacher.'

'No!'

Alexander yelled and threw himself forward as the gun fired, cannoning into the gunman and knocking him off balance. The bullet meant for Connor went wide and then his own gun was back in his hand. He thumbed a shot at the gunman who had brushed off Alexander and was trying to line up his gun again. Under the impact of the bullet the stricken man staggered back and collapsed in a heap. There was a sudden flurry of movement as the men he had originally confronted pulled weapons. Swivelling, he fired into the mob. Suddenly guns were going off all around.

Bullets thudded into the bar around Connor as he fired off his own weapon. Men were being hit with every shot. They were reeling away clutching chest or belly as the preacher emptied his weapon into the men bunched together. His hammer clicked on empty and, without pausing, he released the weapon and it fell to the floor.

Almost immediately his second gun was in his hand and he smoothly continued his barrage. The air was filled with noise and cordite fumes. Men were yelling and falling to the floor, some dead some badly wounded. Connor's second gun clicked on empty and he dived to the floor seeking the gun fallen from the man who had been roughing up Alexander.

As his hand closed on the weapon the noise of gunfire ceased. From his position on the floor he gazed around him at a scene of devastation. Of the sheriff's party no one was standing. Bodies sprawled on the floor amid blood and gore. An eerie hush was upon the salon. Connor climbed slowly to his feet.

'And may the Lord have mercy on their souls,' he said and began ejecting empty shells from his gun.

CHAPTER FIVE

Connor caught a movement out of the corner of his eye and swivelled his gun that way. The pale face of Alexander peered out at him from beneath a table.

'You're safe now, Alexander,' he said. 'You can come out.'

Alexander clambered to his feet and walked over, his eyes wide and staring as he looked at the dead bodies. Connor noticed the bruise on the boy's cheek.

'Are you all right?'

Alexander nodded vigorously.

'That was a mighty brave thing you did. You saved my life when you attacked that gunman.'

The patrons of the saloon, now the shooting had ceased,

were coming to their feet from where they had dived when the action started. Cautiously, they edged to the front of the bar-room, staring at the gory bodies sprawled on the floor.

'Hell, Reverend, you gone and killed Sheriff Taylor and his sidekick Harris!'

'They were one mean bunch of *hombres*,' another voiced.

'What was it all about?' they asked Connor.

'I do regret the killing, brethren. It was not my intention to take the lives of these wrongdoers. But they were threatening violence towards me and my partner here.'

Connor patted the boy's head.

'A family were ambushed on the trail about two days back and murdered. The killers did not know there was a witness to the killings. Young Alexander here survived the slaughter and recognized the murderers. It would seem justice has been meted out, although I do regret it was me as was chosen to be the instrument of retribution, it was surely the Lord's will.'

Attracted by the gunfire, more and more citizens were pushing through the saloon doors and the place was becoming crowded. A pompous-looking man with a small brown moustache and dressed in a dark suit walked up to Connor and stuck out his hand in greeting.

'Wilbur Beaverbrook, Town Mayor,' he said as they shook. 'I regret you had a warm reception in our town. That scum you just exterminated were a blight on our fair community. The Harris brothers were bullies and killers and under the protection of our auspicious sheriff terrorized the town. Sheriff Taylor provided the gang with a safe haven in return for a share of their spoils. You have done this town a great service. Can I buy you a drink, Reverend, or perhaps your calling does not permit you to partake of alcohol?'

'There is nothing in the Good Book to forbid a man to drink liquor. I'll take bourbon and my young friend here will take sarsaparilla. But first I must pray for the souls of those unfortunate men who were led astray from a life of good deeds and respect for the law.'

He moved over to the sprawled bodies.

'Dear God, do not be too harsh in your judgment on these poor unfortunate souls that have gone to meet you this day. Only you can know the circumstances that drove them to be so ornery. But take that into consideration when you do pass judgment on them. And don't judge me too severely either, for I did my best to walk away from this confrontation but these foolish men were intent on harming me and young Alexander here. Amen.'

Connor turned and smiled apologetically at the spectators ogling this strange gunman claiming to be a holy man. Behind him the mayor spoke out.

'Would some of you gentlemen do your Christian duty here and carry these riffraff down to the mortuary.'

There was a bustle of activity as some of the onlookers moved up to carry out the gruesome task. Connor watched them as they worked.

'It sure makes me uneasy to see the results of so much lack of prudence on my part, but more so on the part of the unfortunate folk as provoked the wrath of the Lord to fall upon themselves.'

He turned and sought out Alexander.

'You're a very brave young man. I am mighty proud of you.'

He put his hand on the boy's shoulder and turned back to the mayor.

'Now, about that drink, Mayor.'

'Sure thing, Reverend. It'll be my pleasure. Bartender, bourbon for the reverend here and a sarsaparilla for the boy.'

By the time the drinks were served up, the last of the

bodies had been ferried from the saloon.

'I want to propose a toast to the man who came into Moore and in one afternoon rid the town of the trash that was a blight on our community. What's your name, Preacher? I can't just keep calling you Preacher or Reverend or whatever. You must have a proper moniker?'

'Jason Connor, and this is my sidekick, Alexander Leopold Amery. One of the finest fellas it been my good fortune to ride the trail with.'

'Well, Jason and Alexander, here's to you. '

The mayor tossed back his drink and called for refills.

'Jason Connor, you wouldn't be the same Jason Connor as cleaned out the Barbarossa gang in Cheyenne last Fall?'

'I see my reputation precedes me, Mayor. Yes, I was unfortunate to be mixed up in that messy affair. It is to my eternal regret that a lot of people died during that period of blood and slaughter. I swore to live a peaceable life from then on.'

'Mmm, five dead men ain't what I would reckon as a peaceable way, Jason.'

'You are quite right, Mayor Beaverbrook. When I walked into this saloon I had no intention of killing anyone. A few days ago Alexander's family were attacked and murdered. Alexander witnessed the killing. When we got here he recognized the horse belonging to his family. I came into this place to enquire how come the horse was tied up outside. The sheriff and his friends objected to my questions and became quarrelsome. I was preparing to leave when Alexander come in the saloon and recognized the men who had committed the foul deeds against his family. It was then all Hell broke loose. I truly regret any distress I have brought upon you and your good town.'

'Distress – no distress at all! On the contrary, you have done this town a service and freed us from the yoke of the

27

scum that preyed upon honest citizens. And now I am about put a proposition to you. Set up another round of drinks here, Henry.'

'Hang on there, Mayor Beaverbrook. I appreciate your generosity but we need a meal more than drink. My young friend and I are feeling mighty peckish. Where can we get some decent grub?'

'Phyllis Hargrove runs a boarding house and restaurant over on East Street. I'll take you and Alexander over there and introduce you. Afore that I need to put a proposition to you.'

'Sure, Mayor, I'm all ears, as the buck rabbit said when the cook hung him in his larder.'

'You more than anyone can appreciate now that the town has no law enforcement officer since … *ahem*, since you deposed the holder of the office. You are also a man of the cloth so here is my proposition. You seem suitably qualified to take on the duties of law enforcement and I reckon you would make a very good fist of it. Also we don't have a pastor in Moore. It seems to me it would be of great benefit to this community if you would do us the honour of accepting the dual office of pastor and sheriff. It is the perfect solution. A man of God and a peace officer to boot.'

'Mayor, you do me a great honour and I am at a quandary as how to respond. Can I postpone my decision till we have eaten? And perhaps I could sleep on it. Come on, Alexander, I guess we need to go and see if we can rustle up some grub.'

'Hang on Reverend, I'll take you across and introduce you to Phyllis.'

CHAPTER SIX

The morning was well advanced when Connor and his young charge awoke. On arrival at the boarding house and after being introduced to the proprietor Phyllis Hargrove, a buxom female of indeterminate age, they had enjoyed a dish of beef, roast potatoes and gravy followed by apple pie. As they ate, the mayor had spoken with Phyllis and arranged for them to stay in one of her rooms, the rent of which would be paid for by the town council. On this point the mayor was firm. He insisted this was in acknowledgement of the service Connor had rendered the town by ridding it of those evil elements who had been bleeding its business folk.

It turned out Sheriff Taylor had imposed a tax on businesses in the area, claiming it was needed to protect them from thievery, arson and vandalism. The community quickly discovered it was easier to pay up. Those that did not meet the demands of the sheriff were beaten and their premises smashed up or torched.

The sheriff and his evil cohorts, the Harris boys, were like a malignant affliction on the township of Moore. Jason Connor had ridden in one day and in just one explosive burst of action had excised the canker that had been strangling the commercial life of the town. The citizens of Moore had every reason to be grateful to Connor and, as a consequence, he had been granted the freedom of the town.

'How are you this morning?' Connor asked his young companion, as they tucked into a large breakfast of eggs, bacon and coffee. 'You seem a mite subdued. Though that is not surprising after all you have gone through in the last few days.'

'I guess now you got a job in this town you'll be staying on here.'

'What do you think? I've been offered the double-barrelled post of sheriff and preacher. Now there's a poser for a fella to ponder on. A Bible in one hand and a shooter in the other.'

There was not much talk after that and when they finished breakfast they walked down to the sheriff's office where a delegation awaited them. Mayor Beaverbrook greeted them effusively.

'Reverend Connor.'

The mayor introduced his companions. The banker was there along with storekeepers and ranchers and the top echelon of the town and surrounding district.

'Gentlemen, it is my pleasure to introduce our new town sheriff. The Reverend Connor will play a dual role in the town of Moore. Not only will he keep law and order in our town, but he will also fill in as pastor at our humble church. Already he has shown his sure-fire talents by ridding us of the blight that was hindering our community from growing and prospering. Yesterday he rode in here and, in an act of unsurpassed bravery, rid us of the outlaws that had battened onto the commercial body of our society. We owe this man a vote of thanks and a place of honour in our town. Under the benign protection of Reverend Connor and his cohort Sheriff Connor, we now have the potential to grow and become the commercial hub of the county, if not the state. So what do you say, gentlemen? Do I have the endorsement of the town committee to make this appointment official and offer the dual post of pastor and sheriff to Reverend Connor?'

At the end of the speech the assembly broke into applause. Jason held up his hand for attention, but Mayor Beaverbrook waved him down.

'Wait a moment, Jason! You'll have your chance to speak. We gotta take a vote on this.'

'But I ...'

Before Jason could continue the mayor called for a show of hands to endorse the appointment of the new law officer.

'All those in favour of appointing Jason Connor to the post of sheriff raise your hands.'

The vote was unanimously in favour, with only a few abstaining.

'Look, I ...'

'Patience, Jason, you'll get your chance presently. All those in favour of Reverend Connor taking over the stewardship of our town church raise you right hands.'

Again there was agreement as another show of hands endorsed the appointment.

'That's settled then. The town of Moore is united in its backing of the dual appointment of Jason Connor as town pastor and town sheriff. Now, what was it you wanted to say?'

'The trouble is ...'

'Hold on, I forgot to mention your remuneration. You will be paid forty dollars a month as sheriff. A right generous offer if I might say so.'

'Yes, that is all very well but ...'

Again Connor was interrupted before he could make his contribution.

'Oh, yes, I almost forgot your appointment as pastor. The church runs itself so whatever the townsfolk contribute to your weekly collection will be used for the upkeep of the church and whatever is left over can be used either in sponsoring charitable work or for your own personal needs. All in all a nice comfortable living for any man. And if in the future—'

'Can I just butt in there, Mayor Beaverbrook, afore you go any further?' Connor said forcibly. 'There is something I need to tell you.'

The mayor, unused to being interrupted when in full flow, hesitated and blinked uncertainly.

'Of course, the floor is all yours. I was just going to say that in the event you wanted to take a wife ...'

'I have no intention of taking a wife....'

'... we would provide accommodation for you in that event.'

'And I have no intention of staying in Moore. Beautiful an' all as your wonderful town is, I have other plans which impel me to move on.'

There was a stunned silence. Even Mayor Beaverbrook was lost for words. Not unlike a landed catfish, he opened and closed his mouth a couple of times before any sound issued.

'I don't think I heard you right. Did ... did you say you were moving on?'

'That's what I've been trying to tell you ever since I walked in here. I can't say the offer ain't tempting, but I got other business to attend. So I must thank you for your kindness and generosity and bid you gentlemen good day.'

A babble of voices broke out. Mayor Beaverbrook turned to his townsmen, his arms outstretched in a plea for silence. It took him a while to quieten everyone.

'Leave it to me,' he pleaded. 'I'll persuade Connor to stay and take up our offer.'

When order had been restored the mayor turned to speak to their prospective candidate for the job of keeping law and order, but he stared around in perplexity. There was no sign of Connor.

'What the Hell!'

He rushed outside and was in time to see two riders across the street from the law office start their horses away from the hitching rail.

'Jason,' he called. 'You can't do this. This town needs you.'

Connor angled his horse across the street to stop before the mayor.

'Mayor Beaverbrook, I cannot say I was not flattered and indeed tempted by your generous offer of the job of sheriff, but I have other responsibilities that I must take care of.'

'I'll double your salary,' the mayor said recklessly.

'Good day to you, sir.'

Connor tipped his hat.

'We must be on our way.'

He wheeled his horse around.

'Come on, Alexander. Time's pressing and we have a ways to go.'

'But, but....'

Mayor Beaverbrook was left spluttering as he was forced to watch Connor and his young companion ride down the street and out of the town of Moore.

CHAPTER SEVEN

The terrain stretched flat and low and was surrounded by low hills that trapped the heat and dust. As the horses trudged across the pan, powdery swirls stirred under their hoofs. Soon, both riders and horses were covered in a pale coating of dust.

'How much further, Jason?'

'I reckon another day … mebbe two at most.'

The flat dry land stretched out uninvitingly before them.

'One more camp and then if we push on we should reach your family's farm.'

'They ain't my family. My family's dead.'

The words were choked off abruptly as the memory of the

boy's loss was brought home to him.

'Family is family no matter how far removed. Now what did you say your aunt and uncle were called.'

'Aunt Ellen and Uncle Sidney.'

'And do you mind their surname?'

'It was Amery, same as mine.'

'Your pa and Uncle Sidney were brothers then. There you are – a brand new family to replace the one the good Lord gathered to himself. Do you recall if they had any children?'

'There's Cousin Emma and Cousin Terrence.'

'Well, now, a ready-made family with a brand new brother and sister for you. I know it has been a grievous thing to lose one's close family but sometimes a fella has to take hard knocks. It has often been said that the Lord works in mysterious ways and indeed who are we that are but motes of dust in the order of God's universe to question the ways of the Almighty?'

'Why did he take my family from me?' Alexander said bitterly. 'He's got angels and lots of people that died in the past to keep him company. I got nobody. I think God is selfish and mean.'

'I can understand you thinking like that, Alexander. But there's always a hidden pattern in happenings that we can't understand. God didn't tell those men to kill your ma and pa. They decided of their own free will to do wicked deeds. We all have a choice and those men chose evil. But if you think of it in another way: did God send Jason Connor along that trail in order to help you? What would have become of you if Connor hadn't happened along and took you under his wing? He has sort of become your guardian angel. So though God couldn't stop those fellas from killing and robbing, he sent me along to care for you and then later we went into that town and the Lord told me to punish the sinners who had

34

committed those foul deeds. So God was doing the best he could under the circumstances. He's hindered by the dodgy material he has to deal with. All of us humans are flawed and he works with us to guide and direct us to do the right thing. Sometime we ignore him and do the wrong thing but that ain't God's fault. We always have the choice. If we make the wrong choice then we have to live with the consequences.'

Connor stopped talking and glanced at his young companion.

'Alexander, am I making any sense?'

'No, sir. God made the people in the first place so why didn't he do a better job of it? Seems to me he's to blame no matter what you say.'

'Aw heck, Alexander, we could argue till we are old men and never get the right of it. Wiser men than us have disputed the problem for centuries. So I say we put this discussion to bed and maybe another day we can work on it. It gives me a thirst all this jawing.'

Connor glanced up at the sun, then took his canteen and shook it.

'We need to hit water soon. We're running low.'

He unscrewed the stopper and went to drink, then thought better of it.

'How's your water lasting?' he asked.

'I ain't got none left.'

'Well, then have a sup of mine.'

Connor handed over the canteen.

'Go easy on it, though; we don't know when we'll get to a waterhole.'

Alexander supped sparingly and handed back the canteen.

'Thank you.'

Connor did not drink. He took the water container and

hung it back on the saddle. He stroked the stubble on his face, thoughtfully.

'I hate to go more than a day or two without shaving.'

He grinned across at Alexander.

'That's one thing you ain't got to worry about.'

Alexander rubbed his cheeks.

'I think I can feel stuff growing. Maybe I should start shaving, too?'

'Hey, don't be too much of a hurry to start shaving. It can be a right bothersome chore scraping away at your face with a blade, often as not taking a sliver of skin along with the fur. No, just you put off that undertaking as long as you can.'

Connor pulled out a glass and spent a moment or two scanning the area.

'Afore we go much further I'll see if I can spot a likely campsite for tonight. That looks like a mess of agaves and mescal up on the right there. We'll head that way, and with a bit of luck we'll find a suitable place to stop the night.'

As they rode closer to the copse a few skinny trees poked up into the sky.

'What sort of trees are them,' Alexander asked, pointing to the spindly shapes.

'Bojum trees – kind of rare to find them out here, but where there are trees there should be water.'

The horses picked up their pace as they scented the water. Sure enough, a few hundred yards ahead they came across a shallow pool in a shady area within a grove of trees.

'I'll hold the horses here while you drink and fill our canteens otherwise they'll muddy the water and make it unusable.'

'Sure thing.'

In a short time they had a fire going and feasted on pan-cakes and fatback and beans washed down with coffee.

'I guess sometime tomorrow you'll be with your cousins,' Connor ventured. 'You'll be sleeping in a proper bed and eating home cooking. I kind of envy you.'

'Why didn't you stay back in that town where they wanted you?'

'I won't say it weren't tempting. The pay was fair and the job would have been easy seeing as I had cleared out the troublemakers. And it would have been kind of nice to have a proper church to preach in. But I had already promised to take you to your aunt and uncle. When I give my word, son, it is a binding thing with me. I never go back on it. One thing I hope you never do.'

'I never thanked you proper for looking after things, like burying Ma and Pa and Sis.'

'You don't need to thank me, son. I done what any Christian body would have done.'

The fire burned cheerily and they sat contented before it quietly contemplating what lay ahead when suddenly they both heard a noise. The sound was indistinct, like someone scratching and scrabbling about as if searching for something.

'Stay by the fire,' Connor said quietly.

He picked up his rifle and moved cautiously in the direction of the noise. In spite of Connor's admonition Alexander jumped to his feet and followed. Connor eased stealthily through the bushes following the sound. There came the guttural snarl and a sharp bark. Connor reached out his rifle, parted the branches and stopped. There was still light enough to see two coyotes leaping up and biting at some objects hanging in a tree and occasionally snapping at each other. Connor stopped being cautious and stepped forward. At the same time he shouted out a command.

'Get the Hell away from there!'

Alarmed, the animals instantly whirled round and snarled a warning. Connor cocked his rifle and swung it in an arc.

'Get! Go on now. Get the Hell outta here.'

For a moment it looked like they were inclined to defy him, but coyotes are cowardly beasts and when Alexander stepped out from the bushes they turned tail and scarpered. The two figures hung limply from the end of the rope around their necks. Connor swung around as Alexander came up beside him.

'I thought I told you to stay by the fire.'

Alexander stared with wide horrified eyes at the bodies hanging on the tree, then turned and ran blindly back to the camp.

CHAPTER EIGHT

Connor could hear the boy sobbing. He threw back his blankets and, sitting up, looked over at the youngster huddled in his blanket.

'Alexander?'

The sobbing stopped, to be replaced by suppressed snuffles. Connor stood and walked to the fire, now reduced to a dim glow and stirred the embers into life before replenishing it with more wood.

'You want to sit by the fire for a while? Things don't seem so bad when sitting by a cheery fire.'

The blankets heaved as Alexander crawled from his bedroll and came over to sit beside Connor.

'There are no words of mine that can ease the hurt you are going through. However, I have every hope things will get better once you are delivered to your new family. It was unfortunate that today we camped at the site of such a terrible wrongdoing. No one, no matter what he has done, deserves a fate like that. I have cut those poor folk down and in the morning I will bury them. There is no need for you to be involved. Would you like a drink or something to eat?'

Alexander shook his head.

'No, thank you.'

'If you like, you can lay your blankets by me. It might be of comfort to you if you wake in the night and hear me snoring beside you.'

'Thank you, I would like that.'

'When I was your age, I lost my family also. We lived on a small farm – just my ma and pa and my brother Joseph. He was christened Francis Joseph but, for some reason I never understood, he hated being called Francis and would only answer to Joseph. We ended up calling him Joe, which suited him fine.

'Our farm was right on a river which was handy for watering our cattle and our crops. We weren't rich by any means but we got by. There was always food on the table and we were warm and comfortable and contented. Then our neighbour, a rancher who ran a large herd of cattle, decided he wanted our land and the water rights for his own use. I was too young to know what was going on. Pa did not want to sell up, so one night the rancher came by with his crew and called out Pa and shot him. Joe bundled me out the back door and told me to run to the river and he would join me when he got Ma out. That was the last I saw of my family. I was taken in by an old trapper. Five years later I came back and our house was in ruins. That rancher had taken over the grazing and the water. At fifteen I was a man. I was hired on by the rancher who had murdered my family. Two weeks later I shot him dead. My family was revenged.'

When Connor stopped talking there was a long silence. The two figures sat there – dark shapes in the night highlighted against the glow from the fire.

'That old trapper that took me in, he tried to teach me how to read the Good Book and to live by it. I knew quite well that I was not to take up the gun in anger or in the spirit of vengeance. Vengeance is mine saith the Lord. I felt quite remorseful for what I had done and knew I had to make amends in some fashion. So I joined a monastery and became a holy monk. I was happy there. Life was simple and ordered. But I fear I am a man stalked by trouble. Man walks the earth while the Lord watches, but dark deeds are buried in his heart that are not hidden from the eye of God.'

While he talked the boy slumped against him and when Connor checked he could see his eyes were closed. Gently, he lowered the slumbering boy into a prone position and tucked the blankets around him.

'I guess you fell asleep on purpose so as not to have to listen to me. I never realized how boring my life story was.'

For a long time Connor sat by the fire while old memories stalked his mind.

'Lord, I have shed more than my fair share of blood,' he muttered. 'There are tales aplenty of bloodshed and battles in the Good Book. When David beheld the Philistine Goliath mocking the Israelites he took up arms and went out and challenged the mighty warrior. David slew Goliath and he prospered from that day so I reckon you must have sanctioned the killing. I have tried to take comfort from that tale and shape myself after David. Then I wonder if maybe I like too much the letting of blood. I fear I am flawed and yet I have killed only those whom I considered evil or when my own life was in danger. You have led me to Alexander so I might protect him from further harm. I shall deliver him to his family and then I will continue on whatever path you have laid out for me.'

Eventually, the preacher stretched out and was instantly asleep. In the morning when they had breakfasted Connor told the youngster he would bury the victims of the hanging before moving on.

'There is no need for you to accompany me. Stay here and pack up our camp so we will be ready to move on when I return.'

'I will help you. I am sorry for last night. But it was awful to see those people like that. Why are men so cruel?'

'Why indeed. There was a fellow in England who might have the answer to that. He reckoned we are all descended from animals. He's worked out that apes and monkeys adapted in order to survive and somehow humans were the result. Animals can be right cruel. If you ever saw a pack of coyotes or wolves when they are hunting you would see how they hound their victim; and once they have it cornered, how they rip it to pieces. In fact, they sometimes fall to fighting amongst themselves over the choice portions! That about describes us fighting over the riches of the earth – gold, land, cattle, water rights.... We are animals and have all the instincts of animals. Maybe God shaped us like that so we could work towards becoming good by overcoming our animal natures by sharing and being kind to each other. It's one of the great mysteries of life.'

Alexander helped dig the grave and Connor read over it from his Bible before reciting prayers.

'I've searched them but found no clue as to their identity. I have made a note of their appearance and clothes. When we get to a town I will inform the authorities of what occurred here. One was a young fella not much older than you

– probably no more than fourteen or fifteen at the most. The older fella was in his thirties. They may have been related, but I have no way of knowing. May the Lord have mercy on their souls.'

Connor put up a wooden cross with the date 'May 1888' carved on the cross-beam. It was a very sombre pair that rode from the camp and headed out towards what would be the future home of Alexander and in all probability the parting of their ways.

CHAPTER NINE

The town nestled in a slight depression on the plain that stretched ahead as the two riders crested the low ridge that formed the Magilligan Basin.

'Looks like we're nearly there,' Connor said. 'That's the town nearest your uncle's place. We can get directions and with any luck you should be in your new home afore nightfall.'

They rode towards the town and within half an hour were riding down its main street. Connor pulled up outside the sheriff's office.

'Guess we better report the finding of those two fellas as was hanged,' he said. 'At the same time we can get directions to your uncle's farm. You want to wait while I do this?'

As Connor dismounted, Alexander slid from his saddle.

'Sure, I'll mind the horses.'

Inside the law office Connor found a lean, narrow-faced individual with a heavy moustache and a badge on his vest. He had his feet up on a spare chair as he read a dime novel.

'Howdy, are you the sheriff?'

'Nah, sheriff is Pete Fanshawe. I'm his deputy. Can I help?'

'I found a couple of fellas hanged back at a waterhole about half a day's ride from here.'

'"Hanged", you say. How come?'

'Don't know anything more. I cut them down and gave them a Christian burial.'

'You didn't by any chance know who they were?'

'No, I'm a stranger here. I am just riding through.'

'They have any identification on them, like papers or the like?'

Connor shook his head.

'I searched the bodies afore I buried them. There was nothing to indicate who they were.'

'Could have been suicide.'

'No way! They were strung up high and their hands tied behind their backs. No, they were killed on purpose.'

'I'll make a note of it and tell Sheriff Fanshawe when he gets back. What's your name, just for the record?'

'Jason Connor.'

'Thank you!' the deputy frowned and stared speculatively at his visitor. 'What direction you come in from?'

'Easterly.'

'You wouldn't be the Jason Connor as shot and killed the sheriff of Moore?'

'Word travels fast! I guess that was me all right. The good Lord made me into his instrument of justice so as I was able to slay the wicked men of Moore.'

'Don't try doing anything like that here in Bernville. Our sheriff is one tough mean old coot. He'll have you locked up afore you could get round to shooting anyone. Or maybe he'd shoot you out of hand anyway.'

'What's your name?'

'Deputy Simon Neville at your service.'

'It is not my intention, Deputy Neville, to get on the wrong side of you or Sheriff Fanshawe. I'm here on a mission of mercy and when that is completed I shall be on my way. So tell your sheriff I am not hunting for trouble.'

'Glad to hear it, mister. We run a tight ship in Bernville.'

'One more thing, Deputy, I'd be obliged if you could direct me to the Amery place. I believe they own a farm or ranch hereabouts.'

Connor was aware of sudden wariness that came over the lawman's eyes as he gazed back at him.

'What for you needing the Amery place?'

'I got to deliver a package there, that's all.'

'You know the Amerys?'

Connor frowned.

'No, I don't know them and I'm not likely to get to know them if you don't tell me how to get out there,' he said testily.

'All right, fella, don't get stroppy with me. I represent the law around here and I need to know who is passing through and who is stopping. Carry on down the end of this street. You'll see a trail to your left. Follow that for a couple of miles. You'll see the Amery place away beyond a bunch of trees.'

'Thanks, I'll get out of your way now and let you catch up with your reading.'

The deputy did not respond and Connor concluded there was a distinct change in his attitude since he had mentioned the name Amery.

'Mount up, kid. Another short ride and we should be at our destination.'

The door behind him opened and he saw the deputy step out onto the boardwalk as they rode away. At the bottom of the street before they turned off to follow the directions he had been given Connor glanced back and saw the deputy gazing after them.

'What was your uncle like?' he asked Alexander.

'I don't know. I never met him. Pa wrote letters and Uncle Sidney wrote to him, but that was all. They lived too far for us to visit. It was Uncle Sidney that asked Pa to come and join him.'

'We got to break the bad news to your uncle about your ma and pa.'

'And Sis.'

'And Sis. Uncle Sidney will be glad of a fine, strong, young man like you come to help him.'

Alexander did not answer and they rode in silence after that. When they passed the strand of trees the deputy had mentioned they saw the farm in the distance. As they drew near Connor could make out a couple of wagons parked in the yard and then he saw they were being loaded up with furniture.

'By Melchizedek's beard, that is odd. If I'm not mistaken that looks like a family on the move. Did your uncle ever mention moving on in his letters?'

'Not that I recall.'

'For the time being don't tell anyone who you are until we find out what's happening here,' Connor instructed his companion. 'This is a peculiar development.'

They rode into the yard and Connor hailed the men loading the wagons.

'Howdy, which one of you is Sidney Amery?'

A man in his mid-twenties with a neatly trimmed black moustache and beard turned his head.

'Who wants to know?'

The man's manner was clearly hostile. Connor noted the low-slung twin guns belted around his waist and the way he rested his hands on the butts as he faced the newcomers.

'Name's Connor. Are you Amery?'

'Amery ain't here, so just move on. This property is being vacated.'

Connor sat easy on his horse casting his eye over the yard. He noticed a woman and a young girl standing on the veranda. The woman had her arms folded and Connor could see the tension in her body and the distress in her face. From time to time she wiped at her eyes but there was a defiant and stubborn look about her too. On a sudden impulse he spoke again.

'I guess I'll just have a word with Mrs Amery.'

The gunman flicked his eyes towards the veranda and Connor knew he had guessed right. He nudged his horse forward and suddenly there was a gun pointed at him.

'Mister, I told you to move on. I ain't gonna ask you again.'

Connor raised his hands in the air and at the same time twisted slightly in the saddle.

'Ellen,' he called, 'are you all right?'

It was inevitable the gunman turned to look towards the house and Connor drove his heels into Zipporah. The well-trained horse jumped straight at the man holding the gun. Connor drove the toe of his boot into the gunman's chin and he went down. As he crashed to the dirt Connor launched himself on top of him and snatched the gun from his hand. He stood up watching the man on the ground but also keeping a wary eye on the men working at the wagons who had stopped to watch the action.

'Son of a bitch, you're dead,' his victim yelled, as he scrambled to his feet.

Connor was casually holding the recovered weapon aimed at the gunman's belly.

'I never did take kindly to people pulling guns on me. Now just take out that other gun and toss it in the dirt. Unless, of course, you want to make a try for it and beat this one in my hand?'

Fury and hate blazed from those dark eyes.

'Do you know who I am?'

'Nope but I'm sure you're gonna tell me.'

'You sure as Hell I'm gonna tell you. I'm Seth Leaker.'

'Well, Seth, I can't say as I'm pleased to meet you. You have a very poor way of greeting strangers. Next time you do that someone might just blow your head off. You're lucky this time you met me and I ain't the killing kind. Now, are you shucking that gun or do you want try your luck.'

For a moment Connor expected Leaker to go for his weapon, but Leaker thought better of it. He pulled his second gun and let it drop. The men in the yard had stopped working and were watching the confrontation. Leaker turned and snarled at them.

'What the Hell you looking at?'

The men immediately averted their eyes and continued with their tasks.

'Back up from the gun, Leaker,' Connor instructed.

Sullenly the gunman did as he was bid and Connor picked up the second gun and handed it to Alexander.

'That fella makes any hostile moves just shoot him in the leg.'

Then he walked towards the house and the two females as they stared wide-eyed at him.

CHAPTER TEN

Connor stuffed the gun he had taken in his waistband and removed his hat as he walked forward. He studied Mrs Amery as he came up to the porch. She was a handsome woman, tall, her brown hair tied with a ribbon in a bundle behind. Her face was pale as she looked at him.

'I apologize for using your Christian name, ma'am, afore we were properly introduced but I had to distract that popinjay somehow.'

'You shouldn't have done that. That's Seth Leaker. He's a professional gunman and he's killed several men already.'

'Well, ma'am, I took his guns away from him and here I am still alive. What's going on here?'

'I'm being evicted from my home. You didn't say who you were and yet I heard you ask for my husband. Do you know him or of him? Have you heard anything?'

'Jason Connor, ma'am. Yes, I was looking for Mr Amery. I brought his nephew. Maybe we should go inside?'

'Mr Connor, didn't you hear what I said. I'm being evicted. We can't go in there.'

'We better stop this eviction till I hear the full story.'

Connor turned to the yard and faced the men who had been carrying out the work.

'You fellas stop loading up. I want you to put all that furniture back in the house.'

They stood about uncertain, looking first at Leaker, then back at Connor.

'The Hell you say!' Leaker yelled. 'Any man stops work is fired.'

Connor strode towards the gunman who stood defiantly watching him. In one swift movement Connor pulled Leaker's own gun and swiped him across the head. As the man went down Connor hit him again and he sprawled in the dirt out cold. He turned back to the workmen.

'You got two choices. You can join your boss here in the dirt or you can do as I tell you.'

Sullenly the men moved to obey, dragging chairs and cupboards from the wagons and carrying them back into the house.

'For every broken item I break a few heads,' he called.

In a short time the wagons were emptied.

'Now take your boss and get outta here.'

As they loaded the unconscious gunman Connor emptied the bullets from Leaker's guns and tossed the weapons into the wagon.

'He'll kill you for sure,' one of the men said. 'He's as dangerous as a rattlesnake. He's killed a few in his time. No one can stand against him.'

'He doesn't look too dangerous to me,' Connor commented, as he looked into the wagon. 'He's maybe brave coming out to evict a woman and a girl along with a crowd of lackeys to back him.'

He stood watching the empty wagons trundle out of the yard and head back towards town. After he helped Alexander with the horses they went inside to find the woman and young girl busy putting their house to rights. She turned and gave them a tight smile then came forward.

'You said you were bringing our nephew. Are you Alexander?'

'Yes, ma'am,' the boy said. 'I reckon so.'

She swept him up in an embrace, then stood holding him at arm's length before pointing to the young girl standing shyly behind her.

'This is your cousin Emma. Where is the rest of the family?'

'Please sit down, Mrs Amery,' Connor said. 'I got some bad news.'

Her face paled, showing up her freckles, but she did as he suggested and sat watching him with anxious eyes.

'Alexander's family were attacked by outlaws on the way here and Alexander is the only one to survive.'

Her hand flew to her mouth.

'Oh, dear God! Oh, you poor boy!'

She stared over at Connor.

'Who are you? I mean how come you are looking after Alexander?'

'He killed the men who murdered Ma and Pa,' Alexander blurted out.

'*You* killed them. Are you a gunman – like Leaker?'

'No, ma'am, I surely am not like Leaker. I did kill those men but they were trying to kill me at the time and they had already murdered your brother and his family.'

He could see she was not convinced and sought to change the subject.

'What was happening here today? And where is your husband?'

'I don't know. Sidney and Terrence went to Potterville with a herd of cattle to sell. That was a week ago. They should have returned by now. Then today Leaker came out here and said we had to get out as we owed money to his boss, Steve McLeish. I knew nothing about this money but you saw what was happening. If you hadn't come along we would have been sleeping under the stars tonight. I wish my boys would return soon. I hope nothing's happened to them.'

'Who knew they were going to Potterville?'

'Everybody knew. Sidney was to sell cattle for some of our neighbours. We had forty head of our own and then by the time he left there was about one hundred and fifty altogether. Why do you ask?'

'Just a hunch is all. Could you describe your men folk?'

'I can do better than that. I can show you a photograph.'

She fetched a daguerreotype showing a family group

dressed in Sunday best, posed and formal. For long moments Connor studied the faces before handing it back. She saw the anguish in his eyes as he gazed back at her.

'I need to go outside for a smoke.'

'What is it?'

But Connor did not answer and the woman followed him outside.

'Something's happened to my boys. Tell me what it is. You know something don't you?'

'I don't know how to tell you, Mrs Amery. It's bad.'

The starch went out of her then and she collapsed on to the rocker. One hand flew to her mouth and with the other she clutched at her stomach. She gave a cry like a wounded animal and rocked back and forth. Connor built his smoke and listened to the soft sobbing of the woman and wished he was anywhere but here with the task of telling Ellen Amery of the two bodies buried by a waterhole.

CHAPTER ELEVEN

'Mr Connor, can you take me to where they are buried? I must bring them home.'

Connor had stayed the night. Once Ellen Amery had recovered from the initial shock of her grief she busied herself making her visitors welcome. She had cooked dinner and made up beds for them. After breakfast Connor had gone outside and stood by the yard gate smoking and thinking. He heard her come up behind him but did not turn till she had spoken and made her request.

'I guess I would be best suited to that task, Mrs Amery. It is no job for a woman.'

'They are my boys, Mr Connor. I need to do this for them.'

'You need to stay here and look after those two children. They have suffered much grief losing parents. They need a mother to comfort them.'

Her face crumpled then and for a moment he thought she would break down but she recovered and stared at him with grief-stricken eyes.

'It seems too much for one family to bear,' she said, her voice husky with suppressed emotion.

'I sense strength in you, Mrs Amery. You have a good heart and you will cope and make a fine life for your children. I know Alexander is not your child but he is of your husband's blood. You can make a home here for him and he will grow up knowing your love and the companionship of his sister Emma.'

'You are a strange man, Mr Connor. Alexander told me you are a preacher. Is that true?'

'I do try to preach the Word of God, unworthy though I am of such a calling.'

'And yet you carry guns and you killed the men who murdered my brother-in-law and his wife.'

'I have to confess to such actions, ma'am. It grieved me to have to do so. The Good Book tells us when there are serpents in your house you must remove the offending creatures by whatever means necessary. I make no excuses for slaying those evildoers. I was gravely provoked.'

'And yesterday, when you confronted the gunman Leaker you challenged him to a duel. You would have shot him if he went for his gun.'

'I prayed that he would see sense and go on his way peaceably. Fortunately for us both he saw the wisdom of that and I am grateful to the Good Lord that no blood was shed.'

'You did not shed his blood but you humiliated him in front of those men. He will not take kindly to that. He will come seeking you and when that happens you will have to kill him or he will kill you.'

'I have no control over Seth Leaker's actions, Mrs Amery. If he seeks revenge there will be consequences. Those who live by the sword will perish by the sword.'

'But he might kill you. Have you thought of that?'

'Death is but a step from one life to another life. When the Good Lord gathers me to his bosom, I hope I shall be worthy of his embrace. However, I would like to think I have many years left for me to preach the Word of God.'

For long moments she looked at him.

'Bring them back for me, Mr Connor. I must do right by my men.'

'I will go into town and hire a wagon and maybe someone to help. We will bring your men folk back. When all is ready I shall come for you and your children and we will give them a proper burial. I did say prayers over them at the time.'

'Let me go into town for the wagon. You might run into Leaker and there will be trouble.'

'Mrs Amery, what kind of man sends a woman to do his work for him? Would you want me to hide out here? If Leaker wants me bad enough he will seek me out no matter where I hide. I'll saddle up and go in.'

'What if Leaker comes out here again?'

'Can you shoot a gun, Mrs Amery?'

Her eyes narrowed and she stared back at him.

'You want me to fight Leaker?'

'No, I want you to defend your home and your children. I don't think even Leaker would shoot down a woman and her children. No one would stand for him killing a woman. If needs be, fire a couple of rounds in the air to let them know you are not fooling. But you don't have to shoot anyone.'

'Why are you doing this? You could just ride on. You are not beholden to anyone here.'

'He that helps his neighbour and brings in his animals and stacks his neighbour's corn is doing the work of the Lord and is building upon the glory of God.'

'You are the oddest preacher I have ever come across. But then what do I know of preachers. I can see you are set on this course of action. I have no option but to allow you to go for you know where my poor dead boys lie.'

Connor rode into Bernville past the finely constructed houses on the outskirts with their tidy gardens. He stopped by the imposing stone church and regarded it with some longing but then carried on into the commercial part of the town. He headed for the general store knowing the owners of such places would be acquainted with most of the gossip and who would be for hiring. He hitched his horse outside.

'Listen, Zipporah, don't go getting into any trouble.'

The horse regarded him with a sceptical eye.

'Don't look at me like that. You know I don't go around looking for trouble. It comes looking for me.'

Inside the store were four shoppers – two women and two men. Behind the counter an elderly man and a middle-aged plain-looking woman were serving. Connor drifted to the front and coughed to attract attention.

'Be with you in a minute, fella, as soon as I've served these customers.'

'I ain't here buying. I need a wagon and a man to hire. Thought you might know where I could get the same.'

'You should try the livery. Jude should be able to fix you up. You're new around here ain't you? Name's Harry Webb; this is my daughter Catherine.'

'Yup, I just got in.' Connor tipped his hat. 'Thank you.'

'You ain't told us your name.'

Connor sighed before answering.

'Jason Connor. I'll try the livery.'

At the mention of his name all bustle in the store ceased. Before anyone could speak Connor turned quickly and left.

'Well, if there's gonna be trouble, let it be after I complete my mission,' he told the horse as he untied it.

Zipporah whickered.

'Yeah, yeah, I know.'

He swung aboard and walked the horse down the street till he saw the livery on the right. Inside he found the stableman forking hay into feed bins. He was bent over and Connor assumed it was because of what he was doing, but when he turned to see who had entered he realized the man was set permanently in the shape of a bow.

'Howdy, I'm in need of a wagon and a fella who don't mind handling dead bodies.'

Tobacco-stained teeth grinned out at him from behind a straggly moustache.

'Hee, hee, hee! Who you intend killing?'

'You can rest easy on that score. These fellas are already dead.'

'You come to the right place. I'm the undertaker and I got the wagon.'

'How much for a couple of day's work? The bodies are a half day's ride from here. We might have to camp out unless you don't mind working at night.'

The stableman stroked his moustache, then spat.

'I'll have to hire someone to mind the livery while I'm away. And then there's the hire of the wagon. Nineteen dollars all in.'

'Does that include re-burying the bodies?'

'How many bodies are there?' the undertaker asked

shrewdly, eyes squinting suspiciously.

'Two.'

'Two. Mmm, that'll be another ten dollars.'

'Jehoshaphat, I can't afford that! Tell you what; I'll just hire me the wagon and I'll do the digging myself.'

'Tightwad! Five dollars for the wagon and I'll have to keep your horse here as a deposit just in case you don't come back with the wagon.'

'Connor!' someone called his name from outside. 'Come out and face me. I'm gonna kill you.'

'Connor! Is that you?' the stableman asked.

When Connor nodded the livery man darted to the door and peered out.

'Mister, that's Seth Leaker out there.'

He turned back to Connor.

'Can I have your horse after he kills you?'

CHAPTER TWELVE

Connor removed his jacket. Underneath he was wearing a holstered gun.

'This Leaker fella good with a gun, then?' he asked.

'Nobody better, fast as greased lightning. What's your full name, Connor?'

'Jason Connor; why you need to know?'

'For the grave-marker. You got any dependants, Jason Connor?'

'Nope, there's just me.'

'Connor, are you coming out or are you yeller,' Leaker called.

'Get that wagon ready, old timer. I'll need to get started pretty soon seeing as I'll be doing all that digging on my own.'

'Hee, hee, hee. It'll be me as will do all the digging. You want anything special on your grave? That horse and rig of yours will pay for a good send-off.'

'What's your name? I need to know who it is as is trying to swindle me.'

'Jude Manson – undertaker and liveryman.'

'You mind what I say, Jude Manson.'

Connor groped in a pocket and pulled out a crumpled bill.

'Here's the payment for that wagon.'

The face turned up to him and a frown wrinkled that shrewd countenance as he tucked the money into his own pocket. Connor pulled his gun, checked the loads, spun the cylinder pouched it and stepped to the entrance. Seth Leaker was standing in the middle of the street, feet apart with fingers splayed over his guns. His hat was pulled down over his brow but did not hide the bandage on his head.

'I'm gonna kill you, Connor. You might think you're a big name but very shortly you will become a notch on my gun.'

There was a movement behind Connor and the ostler darted out and untied Zipporah.

'Hee, hee, hee. Don't want him hit by any stray bullets,' he declared, as he led the horse inside the stable.

Connor started walking towards the gunman.

'It doesn't have to be like this, Leaker. How if I apologize for hitting you and we shake hands and walk away friends?'

'No way,' snarled Leaker. 'I'm gonna kill you and no amount of squirming on your part will alter that.'

'How come you knew Sidney Amery would not be at home? You went out all brave to evict a woman and her child knowing there were no menfolk to stop you. Did you know something had happened to Amery and his son Terrence?'

'What the Hell you talking about? I just follow orders. Amery owed money and I had the job of collecting any way I saw fit. If it meant kicking his widow out....'

The gunman stopped, realizing what he had just said.

'You knew Amery was dead because you helped lynch him and robbed him of the money he got for his cattle. Who else was with you that day, Leaker, when you ambushed a peaceable man and his boy? He was a hard-working rancher, not like you and the scum that helped murder him. Terrence was only a kid barely fourteen.'

The street was filling up as the citizens, anxious to witness the confrontation gathered in doorways and at windows and watched from alleyways.

'Shut your mouth and draw!'

'There's a fella on the roof with a rifle.'

Connor heard the undertaker's hissed warning. With one smooth movement he drew his revolver and fired across his body at the head and shoulders of the man outlined against the sky on the top of the building opposite. At the same time he threw himself sideways and rolled to a stop against the wall of the livery. Bullets thudded into the planking above him as Leaker drew and fired.

Connor fired at the gunman from his prone position. His bullet took Leaker in the chest and the gunman staggered back. His guns were in his hands and he triggered another shot towards his opponent. It was not an easy task with a bullet in his chest and the shot kicked up dust out in the street. Slowly Connor stood.

'Throw down your guns, Leaker. I don't want to kill you. I want you to hang for the murder of the Amerys.'

'Go to Hell!'

The gun was wavering as Leaker fired again. Connor's gun flamed and Leaker was punched from his feet. For a moment his boots kicked at the dust and then he was still. Connor swept his gun around towards the roof opposite, then noticed the rifle lying in the dirt.

'Goddamn my toenails if you aren't death on two legs.'

The undertaker was hopping about in his excitement.

'You done gone and killed that Leaker. Someone help me carry him,' he called out to the onlookers.

He turned and pointed a finger at Connor who was punching spent shells from his gun prior to reloading.

'You wait here, Mister Connor. As soon as I've delivered Leaker to the mortuary I'll tend to your requirements.'

Muttering with excitement or some other emotion, the undertaker hobbled across the street to where Leaker lay. A curious crowd was gathering, staring down at the dead gunman. Connor went inside the livery and began to unsaddle Zipporah. He heard footsteps and moved so he was inside a pen. Two men came inside, one carrying a scattergun and both wearing law badges. Connor had his gun out and resting on the door of the stable as they came through the door.

'Jason Connor, you're under arrest for the killing of Seth Leaker.'

The speaker was a muscular-looking man with a weather-beaten face and a moustache. His deputy was long and angular and mean. He hefted the scattergun and bared his teeth in a grimace.

'The shot from this little peashooter will cut you in half if you give any trouble.'

'Not if I shoot you first,' Connor said.

The two men stopped and regarded the man standing inside the stable. The deputy put the scattergun to his shoulder and squinted down the barrel at Connor.

'You heard what the sheriff said – you're under arrest for murder.'

'Murder is it? When a gunnie calls a fella out and has his partner hid across the street to bushwhack him, you consider it murder to defend himself? That ain't the case where I come from. A man has a right to defend himself.'

'Say the word, Pete and I'll blow him to kingdom come.'

'Sheriff, I won't bother shooting your deputy first. I'll kill him after I've shot you.'

'You realize you are putting yourself outside the law.'

'I realize I don't recognize the brand of law you follow in this town. Something stinks here and I aim to find out what it is. Sidney Amery and his son Terrence were murdered and robbed on their way home after selling a herd of cattle. Leaker was involved in that murder and went out to the Amery place to evict his widow. And now you want to arrest me for killing the son-of-a-bitch murderer. Terrence Amery was fourteen. There was more than one man involved in that crime. You would do better to look closely at Leaker's associates and find out who else was involved in the Amery murders. There's a fella with one of my bullets in him as could probably tell you something about it. He was on the roof across the road aiming to bushwhack me if Leaker weren't up to the task. Find him and I bet he'll be able to tell you about those lynchings.'

'Connor, you get the Hell out of my town. This was a peaceable community afore you arrived. Now I got a dead body out in the street. Saddle up that horse and go. Next time I see you it will be across the barrel of a gun.'

The sheriff began backing out of the livery.

'Come on, Jake, We'll let the son of a bitch go this time. Remember, Connor, you ain't welcome in this town.'

60

CHAPTER THIRTEEN

The hearse was being drawn by two fine-looking blacks. Connor thought the only thing missing were the plumes attached to the harness. Beside him the liveryman-now-funeral-director was ensconced in a specially adapted seat, humming tunelessly as he drove them along the track. Earlier when the undertaker hitched up the hearse Connor had blinked in disbelief.

'You expect me to drive out in that to recover the bodies? Ain't you got something less conspicuous?'

'You ain't driving it, Mister Connor. I wouldn't trust you to drive a valuable vehicle like this. I'll be in the driving seat, as Lady Macbeth once said to her husband.'

'Consarn it, Jude, I said I couldn't afford the whole works.'

'You already paid, Mr Connor. Even gave me the five dollar fee up front.'

Jude nimbly climbed into the driving seat.

'I never liked that Seth Leaker. Used to come in the livery and call me dirty names. He would kick and punch me sometimes. You did the world a favour by killing him.'

So now they were driving out to the lynching site to recover the bodies and the undertaker was doing it all for the price of the original five dollars, which had been the fee for the hire of a wagon only.

'You saved my life back there,' Connor ventured. 'I knew there would be some kind of edge where Leaker was concerned, but I hadn't spotted it till you told me where the bushwhacker was holed up.'

'Hee, hee, hee. You are a poor liar, Mister Connor. I guess you seen him all right but I couldn't take that chance.'

'Call me Jason. Mister doesn't set too well with me.'

Jude cast him a sideways glance and they continued in silence for a few miles.

'Jude, I need some information about the set-up here in Bernville. There's something not right there. Who's in charge? Who pulls the strings?'

'The things I'm gonna tell you never came from me. I'm like the pet dog you abuse and kick but otherwise never take much notice of. But I listen and watch and make a note of everything in this little old brain.'

The liveryman tapped the side of his head.

'McLeish is a businessman arrived from the East some time back, don't remember exactly. He had money and he had government connections. He wangled the contracts to sell beef to the army and the Indian reservations. Before that the local farmers worked together and were signed up to those same contracts. McLeish undercut them and took over the business. The farmers were obliged to sell their beef to McLeish or find another market. Of course, he offered them prices well below what they were used to. That was when Sidney Amery ran afoul of McLeish. He organized cattle runs to different markets where they got a better price than McLeish give them. The ranchers in the cooperative had a kind of rota and took it in turns to drive the cattle to what-ever market Amery figured would be best. McLeish didn't like that. In the end he tried to buy out Amery but he refused to sell.'

'Where does this McLeish hang out?'

'He has a place back East and spends most of his time there. I guess he needs to be near the government officials he has to bribe or lobby over the contracts for selling to the army and to the Indian reservations. Occasionally he drives down to Bernville to keep an eye on things. Stays at the Mammoth Hotel when he's here.'

'So who runs things for him?'

'There's the banker Hawley as handles all his finances. Then he also has Sheriff Fanshawe in his pocket. Takes care of anyone as causes trouble over McLeish's business dealings. And until you killed him he had his own pet gunfighter to handle anyone the sheriff couldn't touch.'

The undertaker took out a plug of tobacco and offered it to Connor who declined and pulled out his own makings. While he built a smoke Jude took a bite of his wad and chewed noisily, spitting occasionally over the side of the wagon.

'That's the long and the short of it. You can figure out the rest of the story for yourself.'

Ellen Amery came to the door with her rifle when she saw the vehicle approach. She held the weapon ready as Connor drove through the gate, then relaxed as she recognized the driver.

'Madam, your carriage awaits,' Connor called.

She was looking with some puzzlement at the vehicle. It was a wagonette designed with inward-facing benches in the rear for passengers and with a forward-facing seat at the front for the driver. Connor lifted out a sack.

'I brought some supplies. Coffee, beans, flour, salt and some candy for the youngsters. I hope you don't mind. Can we go inside? I have some news for you, Mrs Amery.'

'I heard the news. My neighbours came by. Told me you shot Seth Leaker.'

'I'm afraid so, Mrs Amery. After I left here to go in town to hire a wagon Leaker braced me. I did not want to kill him – even offered to apologize for hitting him. But no, he was determined on shooting it out with me. I had no option but to defend myself. I am not proud of what happened.'

'They say you accused him of murdering Sidney. Is it true?'

GUN BARREL JUSTICE

'Yes, he more or less admitted to it. But there were others involved. I asked Sheriff Fanshawe to investigate. But I don't have much faith in his doing anything. He seemed more interested in arresting me for shooting Leaker.'

'Mr Connor, I'm afraid I misjudged you. I mistook you for a gunman like Leaker. Alexander told me all that happened to him and his family. You were trying to do your best by him and now you are trying to do your best by me and my family.'

'Ma'am, I'm not a killer by choice. I regret the death of any man. But when you are in the firing line and it is kill or be killed, then I will defend myself to the best of my ability – even if it means the taking of life. I don't reckon I ever shot anyone as didn't deserve it or if it was to preserve my own life or protect innocent people.'

'Please, Mr Connor, I was not accusing you. I merely wanted to confirm the rumours that were brought to me regarding the fight in Bernville. Why did you not tell me how you found my husband and my son? I had to hear it from Alexander.'

'I did not want to distress you any further. It was hard enough bringing you the sad news as it was.'

'What am I thinking of? Please come inside, Mr Connor. Can I get you food or a drink?'

'I ate afore I left town, but I sure could do with a strong brew of coffee.'

He hefted the sack.

'There's coffee here if you are short.'

Inside the house Connor sat at the table while the children unpacked the food supplies. Finding the candy brought a squeal of delight from Emma.

'That was very thoughtful,' Ellen told Connor over coffee. 'I can't remember the last time Emma had candy.'

'Children should be sheltered from the harsh world of

adulthood for as long as possible. Those two have suffered grievously in the past few weeks. I only sought to bring a brief taste of joy into their lives. I have completed the errand we agreed on and the bodies of Sidney and Terrance are now resting at the undertakers in Bernville.'

Her face paled and she took a sharp intake of breath.

'That's what the wagon is for,' he continued, 'to take you into town for the interment. Have you someone who could look after the children?'

'I don't think that will be necessary. Emma will accompany me. I don't know if Alexander would want to come.'

In the event everyone travelled into town – Alexander not wanting to be separated from his new family.

CHAPTER FOURTEEN

Connor pulled up outside the undertaker's and applied the brake.

'Wait here while I find out if everything is ready for us.'

Jude Manson was waiting inside.

'Jason, we got no preacher. The story is he's gone to visit his brother in California. Nobody knows when he'll be back.'

'I got Mrs Amery and the children outside. We can't really delay any longer. Those bodies were ripe when we brought them in. What sort of preacher goes off and leaves his flock high and dry like that?'

'Pastor Robb left shortly after he spoke out against McLeish and his gunmen. I ain't saying it's connected in any way, but it does seem mighty suspicious.'

They heard a step outside and Mrs Amery came in. Jude

hobbled across to her.

'Mrs Amery, I sure am sorry for your trouble. We'll be ready soon. Pastor Robb is away on vacation. I'm trying to figure out if you want to proceed without a minister.'

The woman glanced across at Connor.

'Alexander told us you were a man of God, Mr Connor. Perhaps you could perform the service?'

'I would be real proud to speak for your husband, ma'am. If that is what you would want?'

She nodded then turned to the undertaker.

'Mr Manson, I would like to see my husband and son.'

Connor could see Jude twist uncomfortably as he answered.

'Mrs Amery, I don't think that will be possible. Everything's fastened down. It would be a helluva job to undo it all.'

'I would like one last look.'

'Ma'am,' Connor intervened, 'what Jude here is trying to say, there's nothing to see. The bodies were in the ground a piece and what with the time going on it would not be a good thing to expose them to any more delay. I would advise against it. Remember them as they were the last time you saw them.'

She put her fingers to her forehead and rested her hands across her eyes.

'Very well,' she whispered and turned to leave.

At the door she swayed and put a hand against the wall to steady herself before moving outside.

'Thanks, Connor,' Jude muttered. 'I was scared she was going to insist. Everything is ready. My driver Tom has the hearse loaded and ready to go when you say.'

Connor raised his eyebrows in surprise.

'You ain't driving the hearse?

'Nah. People think it's bad luck to see a crookback when

they are saying farewell to their loved ones.'

'Superstitious nonsense.'

Jude snorted.

'What the Hell, it don't matter so long as the job gets done.'

News must have circulated that the Amery family had arrived, for by the time the hearse had been prepared a substantial crowd had gathered. Tom, who was to drive the hearse, was a solemn, pale strip of a man, not unlike a corpse himself.

Connor drove the wagon behind the hearse with Mrs Amery and Emma and Alexander. The cemetery was just outside the town, and when the hearse stopped at the gates Connor dropped to the ground and helped Mrs Amery from the wagon, along with the children. He was surprised to see the large crowd assembling outside the cemetery. Men were crowding forward to be in line to carry the coffins in far more numbers than was necessary, but no one seemed to mind. The solemnity of the occasion was making everyone behave with circumspection.

Connor escorted the family to the graveside and, taking his Bible from his pocket, stepped up to the open grave where the coffins had been laid side by side.

'I am a stranger in this town and so was not acquainted personally with Sidney and Terrence. I had the misfortune to meet them only in death. From the gathering here today I can only guess at the esteem in which Sidney Amery was held. I am sure that any one of you standing here today on this sad occasion could tell a story of Sidney's kindness and forthrightness. From what I have learnt he was a strong and principled man who disliked injustice and wrong practice. He stood up for fair play and for treating his fellows as equals. I believe it was his idea to cooperate with his neighbours to take the cattle to a more lucrative market. It was his honesty and love of justice that in the end led to his death at the hands of robbers for he had taken a herd of cattle to market and sold them. On his way back with the money from the sale he was waylaid and murdered.

'One of those scoundrels has paid the penalty for this foul deed. Before I killed him, an action which I tried to avoid, Seth Leaker spoke in a manner which led me to believe he had knowledge of the circumstances of the killings of these two innocents. He would have had accomplices. If any of you know anything of these foul murders then speak to me and give me names. Or better still speak to your elected sheriff, Pete Fanshawe.'

There were a few snorts and muttering when he mentioned the sheriff but Connor ignored these. He went on to speak of the tragedy of Terrence Amery's life being cut short at such a young age and quoted an appropriate passage from the Bible. He stood silent while the two coffins were lowered into the grave and men filed past offering Mrs Amery their condolences. As the mourners thinned out Connor spied Jude hobbling up the cemetery path and assumed he had come to help fill in the graves. In that he was mistaken.

'Sheriff Fanshawe is waylaying for you, Jason,' the undertaker said breathlessly. 'He has several men covering the road into town.'

'How many?'

'More than one man can handle. You won't stand a chance if you go against them. However, on my way up here I thought of a way out for you.'

Jude turned and pointed to the hearse.

'If you aren't squeamish you can hide in that. Tom will drive you into town. I got a horse already saddled at the livery for you.'

'I don't like to run from a fight but as Falstaff proclaims in Shakespeare: "The better part of valour is discretion."'

Connor eyed the undertaker.

'I owe you already for saving me. You're piling up my debt to you.'

'You'll repay me by staying alive.'

The hunchback grinned impishly.

'When was the last time you heard an undertaker telling someone to stay alive?'

Connor held out his hand. Jude looked dubiously at him, then reached out and took it.

'No one ever shook my hand afore,' he said in a queer, choked-up voice. Then he turned abruptly to the hearse and spoke urgently to the driver.

He then instructed Mrs Amery to take the waggonette.

'The hearse will follow you into town and park behind the livery where Mr Connor can collect his horse.'

They had hardly left the gates of the cemetery when Sheriff Fanshawe stepped out into the road and held up his hand. Mrs Amery ignored him and kept the horses trotting. The sheriff had to jump out of the way and half a dozen men suddenly appeared with rifles. One of them reached out and grabbed the harness.

CHAPTER FIFTEEN

Mrs Amery sat stiff and pale in the driving seat as Sheriff Fanshawe came up beside the waggonette.

'Consarn it,' Sheriff Fanshawe fumed. 'I ordered you to stop. Why didn't you obey me?'

'Sheriff Fanshawe, I cannot apologize enough. My mind was occupied with other things, like the death of my husband and son. Are you making any progress in the investigation into their killing?'

'I need to search this wagon, ma'am,' the sheriff said, ignoring her question. 'I have a warrant for the arrest of Jason Connor. I guess you realize if you are hiding him it is an offence to aid and abet a fugitive.'

'Are you saying that Connor was implicated in the killing of my husband?' Mrs Amery's voice was rising to a hysterical level. 'What evidence do you have for that? Did you know that gunmen came out to my home and were evicting me when Mr Connor arrived and stopped them?'

Sheriff Fanshawe was getting red in the face.

'Look, ma'am, I'm just trying to do my job.'

Some of the mourners who had gathered on the road were moving up to listen to the confrontation.

'What's up, Sheriff?' someone called. 'You are arresting Mrs Amery?'

'Yeah, what's she done?'

'Must be serious when you need all these deputies.'

'It's only a woman and her two kids, for pity's sake.'

The sheriff was losing patience rapidly.

'Move on, you people,' he called irascibly. 'This is none of your concern.'

The hearse rolled by almost unnoticed. Then it was past and heading into town. More and more people, seeing the crowd on the road and the stationary vehicle with Mrs Amery in the driving seat, were coming up the road to see what the fuss was about. Mrs Amery was playing her part well.

'My husband is murdered and you are accusing me of a crime. What sort of lawman are you? Harassing innocent people while criminals are free to go about their unlawful

70

business?'

'I have to search this wagon,' the sheriff said tightly, trying to restrain his anger.

'Why don't you arrest my children as well? Are you going to hang us like you hanged my menfolk?'

The words were out before she realized what she was saying.

'I had nothing to do with your husband's death.'

There was no disguising the fury in the sheriff's voice.

'And I'll ask you not to make accusations like that or I will be forced to take action against you.'

The crowd of onlookers were becoming restive and angry murmuring could be heard. The sheriff turned on them.

'What the Hell you all staring at? Clear the road.'

He gestured to his deputies.

'Get these people away from here.'

The deputies moved against the crowd pushing them away from the stranded wagon. Mrs Amery seeing her chance touched her whip to the horses and the wagonnette began to move.

'Damnit all, I ain't given you permission to move,' Sheriff Fanshawe snarled.

It took two of his men to grab the horses and stop the vehicle.

'Shame on you, Sheriff.'

'Fighting women and children is all you're fit for.'

The crowd was getting into the swing of things. Baiting the sheriff and his deputies was a new game no one had ever dared to indulge in before. Mrs Amery and her defiance of the lawman was overcoming their trepidation. Seeing the situation getting out of control, the lawman in exasperation raised his rifle and fired into the air.

Several things happened at once. Mrs Amery screamed

and lashed out at the sheriff with her whip. The sheriff stumbled back and fell to the road and his gun went off again, the bullet hitting a man in the crowd. There was an immediate scramble and some of the crowd began to stampede back towards the town.

The horses, already made nervous by the hubbub growing around them, panicked and bucked in the traces and then lunged forward. The deputies attempting to restrain them were dragged along and then gave up the unequal struggle. It was a race to town between Mrs Amery's wagon and the townsfolk. They left behind a fuming, red-faced Sheriff Fanshawe. Connor was waiting at the livery when the wagon arrived. He showed his concern when he saw the white-faced woman in the driving seat.

'Mrs Amery, are you all right? What happened? I heard shooting.'

She was trembling, visibly shaken by her encounter with Fanshawe.

'Yes, yes. I'm all right. We have to go now.'

'Sure thing.'

He led his horse out from the livery, mounted and followed the wagon out of town keeping a lookout on the back trail. When they arrived at the ranch, Connor helped the woman down from the wagon. As her feet touched the ground her legs gave way and Connor had to support her into the house. A subdued Alexander and Emma followed.

'Come on, you pair, get the pot on and let's have some coffee,' Connor told the children as he settled Mrs Amery in a chair. 'You sit there and rest. A good strong brew of coffee will get some colour into your cheeks. Or better still, where do you keep the whiskey?'

A little while later they were all sitting in the parlour with drinks – the adults' coffee laced with alcohol.

'You want to tell me what happened?' Connor asked.

Mrs Amery told him how the sheriff had stopped them and demanded to search the wagon.

'He said he had a warrant for your arrest.'

She then told him she had more or less accused the sheriff of killing her husband.

'I think I must have hit a nerve then and he got very angry and things got out of control. The way he acted made me wonder if there was something in my accusation. Why is he chasing you so ardently? It was you who discovered the bodies.'

'There certainly seems something mighty peculiar about Fanshawe's behaviour. He is trying to arraign me for the murder of Leaker. Yet Leaker was a known gunman and there were enough witnesses to testify it was him as called me out. It is almost as if he sees me as a threat to whatever double-dealing is afoot in these parts. It seems to me you might have poked Sheriff Fanshawe in a tender place when you linked him to the killing of your husband.'

Mrs Amery looked sharply at Connor.

'Oh, my God, do you really think so? Oh, dear God in Heaven! Poor Sidney! My poor boy, Terrence!'

She rocked back and forth, her arms wrapped around herself. Her children, seeing her distress, crept near and she opened her arms and held them close.

'Mr Connor, I have no right to ask you this and I know you have put yourself in grave danger over this matter. There is no way I can repay you for all that you have done already, but I beg you to protect me and my family from this evil crew.'

A pair of grave grey eyes stared back at her.

'Rest assured, ma'am, I'll do everything in my power to keep you and Emma and Alexander safe.'

'Thank you, thank you.'

CHAPTER SIXTEEN

'If Sheriff Fanshawe believes you have smuggled me out of town in your wagon, there is a possibility he will come out here after me,' Connor told Mrs Amery. 'I could leave and camp out somewhere but then I would not be in a position to protect you. So we have to prepare for the worst. If he comes, he will come with a posse. I don't know how many he can rally. Do you recall how many deputies he had with him at the cemetery?'

'There must have been half a dozen, at least.'

'Mmm, there's a chance he might recruit a few more. We have to reckon on anything up to ten.'

Connor walked outside and stood surveying the yard and outbuildings and looked up at the house. It was a sturdy, two-storey building fashioned from solid wood boards.

'We have to hit them so hard they turn tail and run back to town. Can you shoot a rifle, ma'am?'

'Yes, Sidney taught me. He had me shooting at cans.'

'It's an awful lot different shooting cans and shooting at a man as is firing back at you.'

'Mr Connor, we are both of the opinion that Sheriff Fanshawe may have had a hand in murdering my boys. It is the sort of thing he might do. Sidney was not one to beat about the bush. He made it clear he believed Fanshawe was in the pay of McLeish so the sheriff might just want to silence him. The lynching could have been meant as a warning to others who might think to go against McLeish. Ordinary robbers would have shot them and left it at that, or maybe just stole the money.'

For long moments he stared at her.

'Moses spoke to the people, saying, "Arm men from among you for the war, that they may go against Midian to execute the Lord's vengeance."'

'Is there is no mention in the Bible about arming women?'

'There was a couple mentioned – Jael and Deborah helped the Israelites in the battle against the iron chariots of Sisera. Jael put a tent peg through his skull while Deborah rode with the army.'

'What do you want me to do?'

'You'll be at the window upstairs. The front door will be barricaded so they can't come in the house. The children will be up in the room with you under the bed. You will take pot shots at anyone in the yard. But be careful not to expose yourself.'

'I ain't going under no bed.'

Connor looked at Alexander who stood with fists clenched and a defiant look on his face.

'I want to fight.'

'Me, too,' Emma piped up.

Connor studied the determined faces of the children.

'The reason I want you under the bed is because you are our secret weapon. If we are captured, then you come out from hiding and that will distract the sheriff so we can break free.'

'Bullshit!'

Realizing what he had said, Alexander went red and covered his mouth as he stared guiltily up at his aunt. Connor turned to Mrs Amery and saw she had turned her face away.

'You all right, Mrs Amery?'

'Yes,' she said in a tight little voice and Connor realized he would get no help from her.

He turned back to the children. Emma had her hand over her mouth, but her giggles kept breaking free.

'Now listen here, young man …' Connor began as he glared at Alexander.

But that was as far as he got before Emma gave up trying to hold back and burst into unrestrained giggles. In the face of all this Connor could feel his own laughter bubbling up. Like Mrs Amery he had to turn away in an effort to hide his mirth. Mrs Amery gave a small sound which she tried to muffle with her hand and rushed from the room. By now Alexander was grinning widely and Emma was giggling uncontrollably. It was some time before Connor could restore any sort of calm.

'These men who are coming here are very dangerous. It is highly likely they murdered your uncle and your cousin. I am trying to make sure you don't get hurt in the crossfire. That is why I am asking you to hide. If I don't have to worry about you getting hurt, then I can better protect the ranch.'

Alexander stared defiantly back at him. As he studied the boy an idea began to form in Connor's head. He fetched his bedroll and extracted a small canvas bag.

'When I was in Moore I bought some firecrackers. At the time I had thought that when Alexander was established with his new family he could throw a party. Now I think they might have a more practical use.'

He pointed to the crawl space under the veranda.

'When the time comes you hide in there. If the posse gets inside the yard and looks like making trouble, you start lighting these and tossing them out under the horses. With a bit of luck that'll spook them. Nothing like a bucking horse to throw a fella off his aim. But you do nothing unless shooting kicks off.'

'And me,' Emma chimed in.

'Sure thing – that is, if Mrs Amery allows.'

Connor turned to the woman.

'You're going to be on your own for a while. I'll camp out in that strand of trees. The posse will have to pass it on their way from town. When I see them go by I'll follow and challenge them from the rear.

'This is going to be a close run thing, Mrs Amery. I can't see any way of doing it other than us holing up in the house. If we do that, then they can hold us there as long as it takes for them to smoke us out.'

'I think we know each other well enough to use first names, Jason. And yes, I will be okay. I am fighting for my own and my children's lives and I have seen how ruthless these people are, so I will do whatever is necessary.'

Her face was pale but her voice was firm.

'Your Sidney must have been a big man to have married such a fine woman. I regret I never got to know him.'

'He would have taken to you, Jason. He had this knack of attracting only the best of men.'

'I only hope I'll live up to his expectations and keep his family safe.'

He walked to his mount.

'Keep a sharp lookout. We don't know when they will come. I expect it will be soon.'

They watched him ride out towards the trees just visible in the distance.

CHAPTER SEVENTEEN

Connor loosened the girth on his horse and took out the rifle from the saddle sheath. He sat down with his back against a tree and checked the loads and the firing mechanism. He did the same with his two revolvers. As he worked he thought about what lay ahead.

His was a heavy responsibility. He had placed the woman and her children in the firing line and he was not convinced he had done the right thing. He had told Alexander the men coming against them were ruthless and that was the only thing of which he could be certain.

What sort of creatures would rob an honest man and then hang him and his boy in a remote place where they would have remained undiscovered till their flesh had rotted from their bodies and in time someone might have come across a couple of skeletons hanging in a tree? By then there would have been no way of telling who they were for all identification had been removed and Connor knew that this had been done deliberately. There could be no crime proven without the bodies. He took out his Bible and began reading.

"'And ye shall tread down the wicked; for they shall be ashes under the soles of your feet in the day that I shall do this, saith the Lord of hosts.'"

When he heard hoof beats in the distance he stood up.

"'Prepare your shields, both large and small, and march out for battle! Oh Lord, be thou my shield and protect the innocent from the wrath of wicked men.'"

He tightened the saddle girth and walked to where he could watch the trail. He saw them in the distance – a tight bunch of riders – and counted six, seven, eight. Tough odds.

He swung up into the saddle and slid his rifle from the saddle scabbard and waited. The group of riders swept past not riding hard but steady. Connor left the cover of the trees and followed. No one thought to look behind and he kept his distance.

The posse slowed as they came near the ranch house and by the time they cantered through the gate they were at a walking pace. Connor closed up the distance behind them.

No one noticed the rider behind – all their attention being on the house.

'Get your hardware ready,' the sheriff called. 'Connor is a killer. Like I told you, shoot on sight.'

Warily they peered at the house and outbuildings. The place was quiet, with all the doors and windows closed.

'Hello the house!'

A woman's voice answered from within.

'What do you want?'

'I'm here to arrest a fugitive – Jason Connor – a known killer. If you are harbouring him, the penalty will be severe.'

'He's not here. Rode off a while back and I haven't seen him since.'

'I'll need to come in and look for myself. Jackson and Wilding, take a look inside.'

A rifle blasted from an upper window. The horses jerked and the riders began to pull their mounts around as if to get out of the yard.

'Hold there,' Sheriff Fanshawe roared and the riders steadied.

'I ain't allowing murderers in my home. You've caused this family enough grief. I tell you Jason Connor is not here. Now turn around and go back to where you came from and leave decent folk alone.'

'Fire at will,' Sheriff Fanshaw snarled.

The posse needed no further urging and immediately directed a hail of lead towards the house. Inside Mrs Amery was unable to shoot back for she was lying on the floor as bullets flew through the window and smashed into the wall behind her.

They plucked at flowered curtains. Pictures were broken and a large wash-basin and jug disintegrated, spilling the contents onto the floor. She covered her ears and trembled with fear mixed with not a little fury.

'Stop it,' she yelled, her voice lost in the roar of gunfire.

'"The days of punishment are coming; the days of reckoning are at hand. The time of punishment for the wicked has come; the day of payment is here."'

The rifle cracked out as Connor fired into the air, the sound almost lost in the barrage being loosed by the posse. They were yelling and whooping and thoroughly enjoying shooting the house to pieces. A skittish horse pranced back towards the gate and the rider saw the horseman riding towards them.

'It's Connor,' he yelled.

Immediately horsemen were swinging round to confront this new danger. A hail of bullets swept towards the approaching rider. Connor loosed off a few shots, then slid to the ground. He smacked Zipporah across the withers and the horse trotted out of the line of fire. Ignoring the lead rippling the air around him, Connor dropped to one knee and, taking aim, fired into the posse. A man grunted and bent over the pommel of his saddle, losing interest in the fight as a bullet punctured a lung. Another jerked and toppled from his mount.

'Take careful aim,' Sheriff Fanshawe yelled.

His men steadied and tried to aim with more precision at the deadly rifleman kneeling in the roadway.

Suddenly loud popping noises mingled with the gunfire as small coloured cylinders bounced and sparked and cracked and fizzed in the dirt under the horses. Plumes of acrid smoke rose up accompanying the mini explosions. It was too much for the horses already spooked by the shooting, and they began to pitch and buck in panic. Another man tumbled from his horse. His companions were not sure if it was his horse that threw him or the shooting from the marksman out on the road.

'Get the Hell away from here,' Sheriff Fanshawe yelled as he fought his panicked horse and tried to turn it round towards the gate.

Another rider clutched his chest and slumped across his mount. The horse bucked and he was tossed to the dirt. It was then a chill feeling swept over Sheriff Fanshawe. He watched horrified as the marksman fired another shot and someone behind him cried out.

A horse shot past him with the rider slumped over, desperately holding on. Suddenly a rifle cracked from the house and the sheriff felt a powerful blow on his shoulder. Again the rifle spoke and this time the sheriff received a hammer-blow between his shoulder blades. His horse twisted and jumped as the crackers went off beneath its feet and the sheriff was tossed to the dirt. Then, just as suddenly as it had started, the firing stopped – the only noises now were the popping sounds that had so panicked the horses and even those gradually ceased. A figure loomed over the sheriff and he stared up at Jason Connor.

'"They prey on widows and take advantage of orphans. They take away the rights of the needy among my people."'

The light dimmed and the image of the man became misty and obscured.

'Help me,' the sheriff pleaded weakly.

'If you tell me who was with you when you lynched the Amerys then I will attend your wounds.'

'I don't know what you are talking about ...'

The light went out and with it went also the life of Sheriff Fanshawe.

Connor found two men still alive amidst the carnage and with the help of Mrs Amery carried them into the barn.

'Can you get me to the sawbones?' one of them – a

bearded oldster – begged.

'Tell me who was with Sheriff Fanshawe when he hung the Amerys.'

'Almost all the fellows out in that yard. I didn't hold with killing them. But what could I do. I was only one man. I thought we would mask up and take the money. But Fanshawe, he said "no". He reckoned Amery would point the finger at him and he didn't want that. But there weren't no money. We got that bit wrong.'

Mrs Amery was staring at him, a horrified look on her face. She turned and ran from the barn. Connor followed and she disappeared inside the house. He found the children staring in fascinated horror at the bodies sprawled in the yard.

'Emma, go and comfort your mother.'

He caught up the reins of a pony wandering in the yard.

'Alexander, do you think you could ride into town and fetch the undertaker and the doc?'

He watched the youngster ride out.

'"But whosoever shall harm one of my children, it were better for him that a millstone were hanged about his neck, and he were drowned in the depth of the sea."'

CHAPTER EIGHTEEN

Sandown House was a lavish colonial mansion built in the shape of a letter 'L' and surrounded by extensive well-tended gardens. This was the home of Steve McLeish. It was early evening and McLeish, a heavily built man with sandy hair and blue, friendly eyes that could turn icy when the need arose, was entertaining the grand and the powerful.

McLeish was particularly interested in influential people who could further his money-making schemes. He was chatting to a couple of senators who were only too willing to take advantage of his generous hospitality. A servant arrived to inform him of a visitor. When McLeish arrived in the library he found Richard Hawley waiting. Hawley, a tall, elegantly dressed man, was manager of McLeish's bank in Bernville; only one of the banks the entrepreneur controlled in various parts of the country.

'Richard,' McLeish greeted him. 'I trust you are well. Can I get you a drink?'

He moved to a pull cord by the fireplace and ordered bourbon from the servant.

'Finest Kentucky bourbon,' McLeish boasted as they stood by the large window gazing out into the garden and sipping from cut-glass tumblers.

'I have some rather disturbing news,' the bank manager confessed. 'I thought it best to tell you in person as I did not want to commit the details in writing.'

'It is best to be discreet,' McLeish agreed, and he waited for Hawley to continue.

'The bodies of Sidney Amery and his son were found not long after they were hanged. It was unfortunate the person who discovered them was a known troublemaker – a man by the name of Jason Connor. This Connor seems to have set himself up as some sort of vigilante. Suffice to say, both Leaker and Fanshawe are dead.'

'Leaker and Fanshawe both dead! How many men has this Connor fella with him?'

'It appears he is acting on his own. And he has two of Fanshawe's deputies under arrest and they are due to testify against Fanshawe for his part in the killing of Amery.'

'How the Hell did he connect Fanshawe with the hanging?'

'Leaker called him out and there was a shooting. Before he was shot, Leaker let slip he knew of the murders. Fanshawe tried to rectify the situation and went out with a posse to arrest Connor. In the ensuing gun-battle Fanshawe was shot along with several of his men. Only two survived and Connor persuaded them to testify against Fanshawe. Then, to crown it all the town committee elected Connor sheriff.'

'The Hell you say!'

'I tried to dissuade them but to no avail. Not only that but Connor asserts he is some sort of parson and has taken on the preacher's job.'

McLeish was shaking his head in exasperation.

'Dear God, after all the trouble we went to set up Fanshawe as sheriff, and this Connor comes along, shoots him and as a reward gets his job. Then we chase off the preacher who was mouthing off about me, and Connor takes over that job as well. What the Hell sort of man is he? Hell and damnation, I can't let one man stand in my way. Too much is at stake. I have a lot of money invested in that place.'

'Maybe we could buy him off? Offer him a slice of the cake? From what I've heard, he could probably run it more efficiently than Fanshawe ever could.'

'Do it then. The sooner we get him on our side the better. He sounds like one hellcat. Failing that, we'll just have to take care of him the same way as we took care of Amery.'

'Who would be willing to go against him?'

'I got some dangerous men on my payroll. When you have so many irons in the fire there is always the risk that people need to be taken care of. I thought Leaker and Fanshawe were up to the job, but obviously not. I'll set the wheels in motion straight away. Delay could be dangerous. It might just be cheaper to have Connor killed as to try to bring him on board. If he's taken over the sheriff's job maybe he has an angle of his own he is working on. Tell me everything. The smallest detail might be the thing that shows up this fella's weakness.'

When the banker had finished relating the events of the past couple of weeks McLeish stood deep in thought.

'You say he has taken up with Amery's widow?'

'Looks that way. Connor brought in the bodies and then arranged the burial service. Drove Mrs Amery into town on the day of the funeral, then went back out there. Fanshawe went out to the Amery place on the pretence he wanted to arrest Connor for the killing of Leaker. When you think on it, there were eight in the posse and only two survived. How can one man do so much damage in so short a time?'

'Well, his days are numbered. I need the Amery ranch. When the railroad comes I have it on good authority the route should take it through their land. I want to build a stockyard on that ranch to ship beef to the big cities. Selling beef to the army is good business but supplying the Indian reservations is even more lucrative. The agents on the reservations are happy to take whatever beef we supply, tainted or otherwise and they cover up any shortfall. The surplus we siphon off from that is then sold on to the Army but like I say I want to ship beef to bigger and better markets. Everything is nearly in place for the scheme to go ahead. This time next year we'll be making so much money we'll be able to use some of it to get our own men elected senators. I already have a few in my pocket. The sky's the limit as far as I'm concerned. I'll be one of the richest men in America. So no preachifying son of a bitch is going to stand in the way. We buy him off or kill him off.'

CHAPTER NINETEEN

A few days later the banker was back in his office in Bernville wondering how to approach the new sheriff when his clerk knocked on the door.

'There's a visitor for you, Mr Hawley.'

'Yeah, who is it? I told you I wasn't to be disturbed.'

'I know, but I thought you might make an exception in this case. It is Sheriff Connor.'

Hawley sat up in his seat.

'Ah, you are quite right, Mr Benton. Show him in.'

Connor eased into the office, hat in hand and Hawley rose to meet him and gestured towards a chair.

'Sheriff Connor, grab a seat.'

Connor settled in the chair on the opposite side of the desk.

'Howdy, I tried to see you a couple of days ago but they told me you were away on business. I trust all went well.'

'So-so, a banker has many important clients and sometimes I need to visit the more influential. By the way, congratulations on your appointment as sheriff.'

'That is generous of you, considering you were one of the people opposing my selection.'

Hawley smiled and spread his hands wide in an expansive gesture.

'Perhaps I was mistaken. My information was that you had shot the previous sheriff and it seemed rather rash to appoint his killer to take over his job. But I am sure time will prove me wrong.'

'That is very generous of you. However I am not here to discuss my job. I am here on a private matter. An acquaintance of mine was issued with an eviction notice on the grounds her husband had borrowed money and not repaid the loan. I would like to see the paperwork on this transaction, as the person concerned believes there is some mistake.'

The banker formed a little pyramid with his fingers and smiled in his most amiable manner. Knowing the answer he nevertheless asked the question

'Certainly, I will be willing to help to the best of my ability. Who is this person on whose behalf you are acting?'

'Mrs Ellen Amery of the Amery ranch.'

'Ah, Mrs Amery – a tragic accident, her husband dying like that. I have not had the occasion to offer my condolences to the poor lady. Perhaps when next you see her you could perform that office for me.'

'Thank you, I certainly will. But her husband's death was no accident, nor her son's. It was cold-blooded murder carried out by the late sheriff and his accomplice Seth Leaker. Both gentlemen now gone to meet their Maker to answer for their misdeeds.'

Connor traced a small cross in the air. Hawley said nothing, watching the man across the desk, trying to read him and getting the impression of an amiable man open and willing to make a deal if the cards were played right.

'I take it you have a personal interest in Mrs Amery and her property? I believe she is an attractive woman and a widow with valuable assets; attributes which would spark any man's protective instincts.'

'I guess,' Connor remarked laconically. 'I'm sure she might attract a mite of attention from some of the more ambitious males around.'

'And you, Sheriff, might you have more than a platonic desire to protect widows and orphans from those who might take advantage of a woman on her own?'

Connor raised his eyebrows and smiled.

'Maybe. Who can rule out anything in such a situation? Are you married, Mr Hawley?'

'Yes, indeed, Sheriff. I've been married for three blissful years. My bride came to me with a considerable fortune left to her by her father. It was most fortunate for me to fall in with such good luck.'

Hawley could have elaborated more on his engagement and subsequent wedding to a rich woman. Her father, a selfish man, had opposed the marriage, wanting his daughter to stay at home and tend to his own needs. One day, Hawley had confided in Steven McLeish about the difficult situation and McLeish had offered to smooth his path to the altar in return for a large sum of money to be paid when Hawley came into possession of the anticipated riches that his bride would bring him on their marriage. Considering what was coming his way if the marriage went ahead Hawley agreed. A week later the recalcitrant father was set upon by robbers and shot dead.

After a suitable period of mourning, Hawley married the wealthy heiress. Neither he nor McLeish mentioned the matter again, but when the businessman came wanting favours Hawley was wise enough never to refuse, no matter how unsavoury the deal.

'Much as I would like to help you in this matter, Sheriff, I'm afraid I can't reveal details of client affairs to any Tom, Dick or Harry who comes through the door. I would need the lady to present herself or, at the very least, you would need a signed note from her granting permission.'

Connor nodded.

'I figured that would be the case, so I took the precaution of getting such a document from Mrs Amery.'

Connor produced a folded paper from an inside pocket and tossed it on the desk. The bank manager gave a tight smile and picked up the paper.

'I would have to verify this is indeed Mrs Amery's signature. It might take a few days for that.'

For long moments Connor stared across the desk. Under his stare the bank man shifted nervously and averted his eyes.

'If that is all, Mr Connor, I take it our business is concluded for the present.'

Hawley stood and smiled politely at his visitor who remained seated.

'So how come a gunslinger is given access to this debt and when I come in bearing legitimate documentation you deny me the same consideration?'

Connor took the makings from a pocket and held the tobacco pouch up.

'You mind if I smoke?' he asked, and without waiting for permission started the process of rolling a smoke.

'I'm not sure I understand what your meaning is,' Hawley said.

'My meaning is I want to look at the details of this note you hold over the Amery ranch. You see, Mrs Amery reckons the note is invalid. It was paid off by Amery afore he set back from Potterville. We figure Amery was worried about being robbed. In that he was right. However, he may not have figured on being murdered as well as being robbed. Whatever the truth of the matter he paid the money into the bank in Potterville and cleared the note. So where is that money, Mr Hawley?'

Connor scraped a Lucifer on his boot and lit the quirley. He looked up at the ceiling and blew out smoke in a long stream.

'Well, Mr Hawley, I'm waiting.'

'This is something I was not aware of. I shall certainly look into the matter but I'll need a few days to sort it out.'

'Mr Hawley, I'll tell you the way I see things. You own this bank and you know damn well what goes on. I reckon you could tell me right down to the last dime how much money is deposited in this bank and who owes what and when it is due. If you don't come up with the details of the Amery note, I'll have to assume something crooked is going on and I'll arrest you on suspicion of embezzlement and take you down to the town jail and put you in a cell.

'They tell me the circuit judge comes around once a month. I don't know when he's next due but you'll just have to wait for him to arrive and set up court and maybe he might be kind enough to give you bail.'

Connor stood and took out a pair of handcuffs.

'Wait, wait.'

The banker, his face pale, put out a hand as if to ward off Connor.

'I … I'll have a look to see if we can find the note.'

He stood up.

'Don't try to make a run for it.'

Visibly shaken, the banker walked to a filing cabinet and shuffled through papers.

'Ah, it looks as if you are right, Mr Connor. The note has been paid off. I do apologize. I've been away as you know and I was not aware of the settlement.'

'I need to examine those documents.'

'It is all right I assure you. Everything is in order.'

'Nevertheless, I want to see for myself.'

Connor rose and took the papers from the unresisting banker. He studied them and then looked up.

'I see a Mr Steven McLeish was the man who put up the cash for the loan.'

'Yes, we sometimes farm out loans if the bank is short of funds. Mr McLeish is a respected businessman.'

'I see. So in default of the loan the Amery ranch would come into the possession of this McLeish. Is that the important client you were visiting, Mr Hawley?'

'McLeish is a very powerful man. He has great plans for this area. He would welcome a man of your talents into his team. You could become very rich under his patronage.'

At that, Connor walked to the door, opened it, then turned and looked back at the banker.

'No man can serve two masters: either he will hate the one, and love the other, or else he will hold to the one, and despise the other. Ye cannot serve God and mammon.'

With that he left.

'And I say onto ye,' the banker said into the empty room. 'He who is not with me is against me. Ye have dug thy grave, my friend, and we shall ferry ye into it.'

CHAPTER TWENTY

Once again the banker had to report back to his master.

'He is but one man,' Hawley told McLeish. 'He can be easy to deal with. You said you had some very dangerous men in your employ.'

'Indeed. One man, you say. Then he will be taken care of. My plans are too far advanced to let some do-good, preaching lawman stand in the way. He is but a deer tick to be flicked aside and squashed. Then we can put pressure on the Amery woman and get her to sign over the ranch. The whole scheme hinges on that ranch. The railroad is bound to take the route between Bernville and the Amery place. That ranch will make an ideal railhead to ship cattle and goods. Whoever owns that property can state his own terms and dictate the way development will take place. We'll be very rich men come this time next year. Go back to Bernville and keep an eye on Connor. I need to know who he associates with and what his habits are. Every man has a weakness, whether it's women or booze or money. Find out what Connor hankers after. We may need an edge to get him out of the game.'

Once the banker had left McLeish sent for his coach and a few hours later arrived at a roadhouse in Nasby. Inside was a seething den of gambling men and gaudy women. Music was provided by a four-piece band comprising a concertina, violin, banjo and piano, all belting out music non-stop. The atmosphere was thick with tobacco smoke and noise.

McLeish went directly to the faro game and placed a hundred dollar bill in the table. The faro dealer was a tall, slim woman with jet black hair hanging straight around her pale narrow face. She was extremely beautiful and she glanced briefly at the newcomer when he lost his stake. Relinquishing her place to another dealer, she came over to McLeish and embraced him warmly, then escorted him to a rear room where a card game was taking place.

The faro dealer went over to a man who might have been her male twin for he had similar black hair and pale features. She bent and whispered in his ear. The gambler looked up and nodded briefly at McLeish. A while later all three were gathered upstairs in a private room.

'I need your services,' McLeish stated, after the greetings were finished. 'I got trouble in a place called Bernville. A fella by the name of Jason Connor has killed some of my employees and taken over the job of sheriff.'

'Who did he kill?'

'Pete Fanshawe and Seth Leaker. Fanshawe was sheriff till Connor killed him after he had shot Leaker.'

'They were two tough *hombres*. Jason Connor, you say? What do you know about him?'

'He claims to be a preacher and from what information I could get he was sheriff for a while up in Cheyenne. He then came into a town called Moore and gunned down the sheriff and his deputies. Apparently they offered him the job of sheriff but he turned it down. Since then he's showed up in Bernville, where he pulls the same trick and is now sheriff.'

'I guess it's logical. If you're good enough to take on the sheriff then it figures you're good enough to take on his job. I guess he must have scared the crap out of the townsfolk and they had to give him the badge.'

'And you can't buy him off like you usually do?' asked the woman.

'We have tried but I figure he has some angle of his own. I need to take over a certain property, which was a process I thought was done and dusted when this Connor fella muscles in and queers the deal. How the Hell he got wind of the dodge, I don't know. Perhaps we have a leak somewhere? I wonder about my pet banker down there. My guess is Hawley brought him in with an idea of cutting me out and taking on the project for himself. Can you believe the perfidy of some people?'

'So you want us to mosey down to Bernville and take out this sheriff? What protection do we have in case the law comes after us?'

'Shouldn't be a problem. The banker Hawley will vouch for you. Any further difficulties I can smooth them out from my end.'

'The usual terms?' the gambler asked.

'Two thousand now and another thousand when the job's done,' McLeish said. 'I want no hiccups. You two go down there, fix Connor and I will have a suitable candidate set up ready to step into his shoes.'

They shook hands all round and then the gambler poured drinks. The woman sidled up to the businessman and stroked his face with her long, pale fingers.

'Are you staying for some fun, Steven?'

He smiled back at her.

'I don't mind if I do. I could do with a little relaxation after all the bother I've been getting over this Bernville thing. The sooner it's settled, the happier I'll be.'

She pressed up against him and kissed him full on the lips.

'I know the very thing that will take your mind off your worries.'

'You know, I feel a lot happier now that you are taking on this job. I sure as Hell am glad you are in my employ. I wouldn't want you and your brother coming after me, Sylvia. No hick sheriff is going to last long against such a deadly combination. You and your brother Sylvester have never let me down yet.'

'I have a bed next door. I'll do my best to let you down on that.'

Later that night the coachman was roused from his slumber inside the coach and ordered to drive his boss back home. As the vehicle drove along Steven McLeish lit a cigar and stretched out his legs and gave a contented sigh.

'Sylvia and Sylvester Gurney – known in some places as the Silver Angels,' he growled into the empty carriage. 'I hope that preacher fella Connor appreciates being sent to his Maker by a duo of deadly angels.'

CHAPTER TWENTY-ONE

Connor looked up as the door opened and he leaned back in his chair, relaxed but alert as the two strangers entered.

'Howdy, Sheriff.'

The woman spoke in a soft, husky voice that sent prickles up the new sheriff's spine.

'Howdy, ma'am. How can I help you?'

'We just got into town and thought we might introduce ourselves,' the man said.

His voice was soft and sibilant, making Connor think of a snake uncoiling lazily just before striking and the image made him even more uneasy. There was something about this pair that raised his hackles and he wasn't sure what.

'Right sociable of you folk,' he answered. 'It's a nice peaceable town. You should enjoy your stay here. What is your business?'

They had separated and moved apart almost at each corner of the room and all the time watching him like a couple of deacons sizing him up for some sacrificial ritual. Connor shook his head to clear it of the bizarre notions.

'"Peaceable", you say,' the man said. 'We heard different, sheriff. There we were, hoping we were arriving in a quiet, law-abiding town.'

'Correct us if we are wrong but someone told us the sheriff's job here in Bernville was perilous,' the woman remarked.

And so it went as if they wanted to confuse him by speaking alternatively from each corner of the office.

'They say the previous officer was shot dead.'

'They also say the man who shot him took over the badge.'

'Is this tale true, Sheriff, or is it a fable?'

'Just state your business,' Connor broke in. 'You're making me dizzy with all these questions.'

'Oh, Officer, are you easily made dizzy? That is most interesting.'

'It could be a mite dangerous to have fits of dizziness. In these days of killings one needs one's wits about them.'

'You're a vaudeville act,' Connor concluded. 'If you let me know when it is to be performed I shall make a point of coming to see it. But I can't promise to stay awake for the full act. I have a very low attention span.'

'Oh, when we perform you will stay awake – at least for the first part of the performance. After that, who knows? It certainly won't be boredom you'll die of.'

'Thanks for the warning. I believe you said you came in to introduce yourselves. But I haven't heard any names yet.'

'Oh, I must apologize for the oversight. I am Sylvia Gurney.'

'And I am Sylvester Gurney.'

'Enjoy your stay in Bernville, Sylvia and Sylvester. Now, if you don't mind, I have work to do.'

Connor stood up, his alarm sensors twitching as he eyed up the odd pair. He could not make out if they were a couple or brother and sister, and he did not care to ask.

'I hear there is a rival do to our performance in Bernville.'

'Yeah, and what's that?'

'I believe you do a pretty mean performance as preacher. We'd like to see that.'

'By all means. Everyone is welcome. I'll look forward to seeing you at the church on Sunday. Do come early for it is usually standing room only.'

Sylvia clapped her hands.

'Oh, I can't wait. I trust it is not too solemn.'

'I promise to fill your mouth with laughter, and your lips

with shouting, as the psalmist says.'

Smiling, they left, leaving Connor staring thoughtfully after them.

'I have the uneasy feeling that pair have been sent here to deal with me,' he mused aloud. 'They seem to know what's been going on here. Someone briefed them before they sashayed in here.'

He left the office and wandered down to the livery where he found Jude.

'Couple of strangers arrived in town. Do you know anything about them?'

'Booked into the Mammoth Hotel as Sylvester and Sylvia Gurney. I figure they might be gamblers. Saw them go in the Golden Egg saloon. Why do you ask?'

'My sixth sense tells me they are more than they seem. I have a feeling they're a pair of spies and have been sent here to deal with a certain sheriff who's thwarted McLeish's plans to get hold of the Amery ranch. That ranch is important for some reason. I need to find out why. I think I'll take a trip to the county offices and do some research; maybe come up with something useful. Saddle my horse. And keep an eye on those two for me. I want to know who they meet and where they spend their time.'

As he turned to leave, Connor paused.

'And can you recommend anybody to act as deputy for me? I have those buddies of Fanshawe's in the cells and I need someone to mind the jailhouse while I'm out of town.'

'Sure thing. What about Tom Banner? He drove the hearse for Mrs Amery and ferried you past the ambush at the cemetery. He's reliable.'

After swearing in Jude's man, Connor rode out of town with the intention of visiting Ninewells, the county seat where companies wanting to do business within its boundaries would have to register their interests. The recorder's office was closed when he arrived so he put up at the hotel and spent a quiet night drinking and listening to the gossip, learning nothing of interest. Next morning after he had breakfasted he went to the sheriff's office and introduced himself. The sheriff was a stern-looking man with receding hair line and deep-set eyes and a walrus moustache.

'Howdy, what brings you across this way?'

'I'm here on private business – looking at some property deeds.'

'What was your name again?'

'Jason Connor, and you are?'

'Charlie Jefferies.'

Jefferies squinted up at his visitor.

'I heard about you. You got a reputation for shooting lawmen. I sure as Hell hope you ain't thinking of making a play for me.'

'Charlie, I ain't ever picked a fight with anyone. They all come after me. There's not a killing I don't regret. I try to talk them out of it; that there is another way without resorting to the gun.'

Connor shook his head regretfully.

'You live by the gun, you die by the gun, is how I figure it. Sheriff Fanshawe came after me. I reckon he was acting under orders. I had no option but to defend myself.'

'Way I heard it there were twenty men in the posse as were sent out and you gunned them all down.'

'Whoa!'

Connor threw up his hands.

'Maybe half a dozen and I had a little help plus the fact that two of them survived to testify against Fanshawe. Something rotten is going on in Bernville and I've come over to check out some facts and figure out what that something is.'

'Connor, you strike me as being a pretty square kind of fella. I never did like Fanshawe. He struck me as being a mite too ready with his gun. He had a mean reputation. If I can be of any help I'll do what I can.'

'Had some strangers ride in a couple of days ago – name of Sylvia and Sylvester Gurney. They struck me as being a pretty rum pair. I wonder if you have anything on them.'

Jefferies stroked his moustache while he thought it over.

'Those names don't strike a chord with me. When my deputy turns up I'll have him look through the "Wanteds" – see if he turns up anything. How long you gonna be in town?'

'Only as long as it takes to check my hunch at the land office.'

'Call in afore you leave. See what we have for you.'

When Connor rode out of Ninewells that afternoon he had an inkling of what was so important about the Amery ranch and which made sense of much of what had happened. Regarding the strangers who had arrived in Bernville, he had learned nothing. As far as Sheriff Jefferies could ascertain they were not on any 'Wanted' posters. This did not reassure Connor in any way and he rode back to Bernville, keeping a watch on his back trail and alert for likely ambush spots.

CHAPTER TWENTY-TWO

Tom Banner pulled out a dog-eared book, put his feet up on the sheriff's desk and began to read.

'*Moby Dick* by Herman Melville,' he read, speaking the words aloud, "Call me Ishmael. Some years ago, never mind how long precisely, having little or no money in my purse and nothing particular to interest me on shore, I thought I would sail about a little and see the watery part of the world."'

It was a laborious process as he traced the words with his finger and read slowly. He had been deputized to tend the jail while Sheriff Connor was away. His instructions were to tell no one of the sheriff's whereabouts but to hint he was somewhere nearby. Tom read undisturbed for a goodly part of the evening until he was interrupted by a hammering on the door and someone outside calling for the sheriff. Tom unlocked the door and found an agitated citizen on the doorstep.

'Goddamnit, what the Hell's up?'

'We need the sheriff. There's trouble down at the Golden Egg. There's a gambling fella fixing to kill someone over a card game.'

'The sheriff ain't here. I'm only deputizing for him, minding the jail.'

'Tom, you gotta come. At least you can try and talk to him. Try to talk sense into him.'

'Hell's blazes,' the temporary deputy grumbled. 'I ain't qualified for that.'

'You got a badge. Maybe he'll respect that. Come on, Tom. You gotta do something else or there'll be murder committed.'

Grumbling and cussing, Deputy Tom Banner left the jail and went down to the saloon to find a black-garbed stranger waving a pistol around and threatening to shoot the men sitting at the card table.

'Now see here,' Tom began. 'What's all this about?'

'Don't come any closer, Sheriff,' Sylvester warned, 'or I'll start shooting.'

Secretly flattered to be mistaken for the sheriff, Tom walked to the bar.

'Okay, fella. Can I buy you a drink? I always think as many a problem is solved over a friendly drink. A whiskey for me and – what's yours, fella?'

Down at the abandoned jail, Sylvester's sidekick Sylvia tested the front door and, finding it unlocked, slipped inside. She searched the desk, found a bunch of keys, then walked to the cells at the rear of the office where she found two prisoners. These were the members of Fanshawe's posse who were now awaiting trial over the murders of the Amerys and the raid on their house. In return for a lighter sentence, they had agreed to reveal the extent of Sheriff Fanshawe's involvement in the murders. The prisoners looked up in some surprise at their visitor. Sylvia gave them her best smile.

'Howdy, fellas, I guess this is your lucky night.'

She unlocked the cell door and opened it wide.

'I'm here to take you to a safe place.'

Their faces brightened as they looked with some wonder at this surprising turn of events. Up till then they had been anticipating a number of years in the state prison. Now an angel had appeared to transport them to freedom.

'Hell's bells, that's great news!'

'How the Hell did you manage this?'

Sylvia put her finger to her lips.

'No questions. I'm being well paid to take you to safety.'

The two men came out, one of them limping from a wound he had received during the raid on the Amery ranch.

'No noise. My partner will bring the horses. We'll wait out back till he arrives.'

No one saw them emerge as the prisoners left the jail and slipped down the side of the building with Sylvia coming behind them. The street was deserted. Anyone who might have been about was further down the street at the Golden Egg, not wanting to miss the drama taking place there.

'We'll wait here. My partner shouldn't be long.'

In the gloom of the alleyway the men did not notice the stiletto in their rescuer's hand.

'Who's springing us anyway?' asked one.

'Some businessman; said as he couldn't have you revealing anything at your trial.'

He groaned as the stiletto slid into his side. She was holding him upright.

'What's the matter?' she asked, and allowed him to slide to the dirt.

'Bill, goddamn it, Bill, what's up?'

The second man bent over his partner and felt a punch on the back as the deadly spike was driven in with such force it went all the way through and punctured his heart. With a choking grunt he collapsed beside his partner. Sylvia giggled as she regarded her handiwork.

'Dead men tell no tales.'

She was still giggling as she wiped her blade on their clothing before sheathing it.

Casually, she emerged from the alley and strolled up the street to the Golden Egg. Inside the stand-off was still going on. The deputy was pleading with the gambler to calm down and assuring him there would be no further action taken against him.

'Sheriff Connor is a reasonable man. As long as no one is hurt he'll just put it down to a misunderstanding.'

Sylvia entered the saloon and walked over to her partner.

'Sylvester, what on earth are you doing?'

'These goddamn hicks accused me of cheating. I've never cheated at cards in my life.'

'Put that gun down,' she ordered. 'I'm sure we can settle this without violence.'

She turned to the hapless Tom.

'Where is that Sheriff Connor? I hear he's killed a few people since becoming sheriff. I don't want him coming in here and shooting Sylvester.'

'The sheriff ain't killed anyone since being elected. It was afore when the previous Sheriff Fanshawe tried to kill him as Connor had to do his shooting. And he ain't here at the moment. I'm in charge and I don't want no shooting.'

Sylvia turned back to her partner.

'Come on, Sylvester,' she pleaded. 'Can't we settle this peaceable afore the sheriff gets back? I like this town. I'm tired of moving from place to place. I would like to stay a little longer. I don't want to be run out of town when Sheriff Connor gets back.'

Sylvester scowled back at her.

'Hell, all right then. If these fellas apologize for hurting my feelings, I'll agree put up my gun.'

'Sure, fella,' the four men who had been under threat chorused. 'We didn't mean to upset you.'

While everyone held their breath, Sylvester's face and lips twitched for a few seconds. Slowly he holstered his gun.

'Let bygones be bygones,' he said amiably.

He turned to Deputy Tom Banner.

'I'll have that drink you offered to buy me, Sheriff.'

A collective sigh of relief ghosted through the saloon.

'Here's to peace and prosperity in Bernville,' Tom Banner toasted, feeling mighty satisfied at a peaceful ending to the crisis.

'Amen,' Sylvester endorsed the sentiment and raised his glass.

CHAPTER
TWENTY-THREE

Connor stood in the mortuary and, drawing back the sheet, looked down at the body. Opposite him was Jude in his official capacity of undertaker.

'Stab wounds, you say?'

'One went up under the ribs and pierced the heart. From the small amount of bleeding I would say he died almost immediately. The other fella had a puncture wound in his back and again it would have gone right through to the heart. Someone with great expertise committed these murders. There was no sign of a struggle so they must have known the attacker and trusted him.'

'What sort of weapon would you say?'

'A long thin steel blade like a bayonet or stiletto.'

Connor thought for a moment. 'So Tom was lured out of the jail and, while he was dealing with a disturbance in the Golden Egg, someone springs our two prisoners, takes them around the back and murders them. The only witnesses that might have connected McLeish and Fanshawe to the murder of the Amerys are then quietly disposed of.'

Jude gazed shrewdly at Connor.

'McLeish – how could they incriminate him?'

'They couldn't. It was all very tenuous, but McLeish couldn't take that chance. So he sent in his assassins to make sure they did not testify.'

'You think it was the Gurneys?'

'Who else? Sylvester kicks off in the saloon; Tom is tricked into leaving his post at the jail. Sylvia comes in, frees the prisoners and murders them. These fellas would not have suspected a woman to be a killer. She stabs them, then saunters back to the saloon to deactivate Sylvester.'

For long moments Connor stared at the dead bodies.

'What is it, Jason?' Jude asked. 'There's something niggling you.'

'I'm thinking these fellas are not the only ones that pair have their sights on.'

Jude's eyes widened.

'You think they'll come after you?'

'Maybe. McLiesh's schemes were all in place till I came along and tossed my bola amongst his hirelings. I stopped the eviction of the Amerys and established the fact that Sidney and his son were murdered. Because of all that has happened he can't very well have Mrs Amery murdered or suspicion might naturally fall on him. However, if he gets rid of me there's no one to stand in his way when he puts pressure on the Amery family to sell up or move out.

'Yes, I have every reason to believe that unsavoury duo have the task of clearing any obstacles out of the way so McLeish can take over the Amery ranch.'

'What you gonna do?'

'The assassins used a knife or a stiletto. Maybe that's their preferred method and they'll maybe try to kill me in the same way.'

Connor stared thoughtfully at the undertaker before speaking again.

'You got any old saddles you willing to sell me?'

'Don't know about selling. Got some worn out ones as ain't worth much you can have for free.'

The Sunday service was over and Connor, dressed in a broad-cloth suit which looked out of character and was grossly ill-fitting on him stood outside the church as the congregation filed past. It had been a big turnout as the people of Bernville wanted to see how the new preacher conducted himself. For his sermon he had chosen Exodus 20:17.

'"Thou shalt not covet thy neighbour's house, thou shalt not covet thy neighbour's wife, nor his manservant, nor his maidservant, nor his ox, nor his ass, nor anything that *is* thy neighbour's."'

It had been a poorly disguised attack on the people who had murdered the Amerys and tried to steal their property. The gambling couple who Connor suspected of having murdered his prisoners and that he was convinced were plotting his death had been in the church, also, and as the crowd thinned out they came up to him.

'Mighty fine sermon, Sheriff. Though I suppose you are a better preacher than you are a sheriff. We heard the terrible news of how those prisoners in your care were taken out and foully murdered. We hope you catch the people who did such a dreadful thing.'

'Are you any nearer finding out who did it?'

'Yes, I am very hopeful. There was a witness but he's terrified he might end up just like my prisoners with a knife in the guts. I have to assure him that I can keep him safe.'

Connor might have missed the flicker in the eyes of his listeners only he was watching for it. Any doubts he might have had regarding the identity of the killer dissolved in that moment as he glimpsed an almost feral look in the female's eyes.

'Really, how fortunate. That is a lucky break.'

'It certainly is. As soon as I get my witness to a safe place he reckons he'll give me a sworn statement which I can take to the judge, who'll then make out a warrant for the arrest of the murderer. I should have the case wrapped up in a day or two.'

'Anyone in particular he point the finger at?'

'He won't say till he feels he's safe from the assassin's knife. I gotta move fast in case he changes his mind.'

'Care to have a drink with us, Sheriff? Might help you to relax over a quiet game of cards.'

'That's mighty sociable of you. I reckon I need relaxing. This last while has been mighty troublesome.'

'Great. Let's go.'

In the Golden Egg, Sylvester insisted on buying the drinks and they settled down at one of the tables. The gambler produced a pack of cards and while he shuffled it was obvious Connor was not comfortable as he shifted around in his chair and tugged at his ill-fitting suit jacket.

'I see you ain't used to wearing suits, Reverend,' Sylvia said. 'You look as comfortable as a buffalo in a coonskin hat.'

Connor grinned back at her.

'The suit ain't mine. I had to borrow it. Maybe when I have the money I'll buy one that fits.'

She giggled.

'Poker all right with you, Sheriff?' Sylvester asked.

'Sure, but not for big stakes. A sheriff's salary doesn't run to such expensive pastimes.'

'At the risk of offending you, Sheriff,' Sylvester observed. 'You seem a mite uncomfortable in that suit. Why don't you ditch the jacket while we play?'

'Any other day I would say yes but today is dedicated to the Lord and I promised my mother I would always dress respectful on the Sabbath.'

The cards skimmed across the table as Sylvester dealt. There were only three players – Connor and the Gurneys.

'Tell me something. I'm a mite curious about the relationship between you two,' Connor asked, as he examined his cards. 'I couldn't figure if you were man and wife or brother and sister.'

Connor was looking at Sylvia as he spoke. She gave him her most seductive smile.

'Were you thinking of making a move on me, Sheriff, or can I call you Jason?'

'I'd be flattered.'

'You didn't answer my question. Are you hoping to have a piece of me?'

'Somehow, I don't think a small-town sheriff like me would stand a chance with someone in your league.'

Sylvia laughed delightedly.

'You are too modest, Jason. You're obviously a big wheel in this community. Not only are you sheriff but the preacher, too. Surely a winning combination for any woman. But there again I was told you had set your cap on another; a rich widow with property.'

Connor pursed his lips and shook his head.

'Again out of my league. And anyway I'm not ready to settle down yet. Still got a lot of travelling to do.'

CHAPTER TWENTY-FOUR

As the game progressed Connor won steadily till he was ahead by about twenty-five dollars. Because he was losing Sylvester was becoming more and more surly.

'Son of a bitch,' he muttered once or twice.

Connor could see the signs and reckoned something was being plotted. Sylvester would pick a fight over the cards and with Sylvia sitting to one side of him she would be in a position to use either a blade or a gun to strike while he was distracted by the gambler. Once she had disabled him, Sylvester would finish him.

'Hell damnit, I'm losing hand over fist here,' Sylvester said crustily. 'How about we raise the stakes? Maybe I can recover some of my money.'

Connor shrugged.

'All right with me. It must be my lucky day.'

After a few more games the sheriff was another thirty dollars richer. Sylvester stared steadily across the table at Connor, his eyes mean and dangerous.

'Sheriff, I'm a professional gambler and I know the run of cards better than most. It seems to me your run of luck is something else again.'

'I do believe you are right. The Lord looks after the righteous so I guess I must be doing something right.'

'I suspicion you are maybe giving the Lord a helping hand.'

'If you mean I am a better poker player than I profess to be then that's applesauce. I never had the time or the inclination to indulge in perfecting any skills in that direction.'

'That's not what I mean.'

Sylvester had become cold and deadly and tensed like a snake ready to strike. Connor imagined he was dealing with two deadly snakes that had manoeuvred him into a killing zone. He knew all along what Sylvester was suggesting, but had chose to sidestep him by pretending not to understand.

The gamblers wanted the killing to look like an argument over a card game. They would shoot him or knife him or both and then plant cards on his body to make it look as if he had been cheating. The fact that he had been winning was a clever strategy engineered by Sylvester to make the cards run in Connor's favour.

Connor went along with it, waiting for the drama to play

itself out. He leaned back in his chair appearing relaxed and at ease. He knew the crisis point had come. What happened in the next few minutes would decide his fate.

'What exactly do you mean, Sylvester?'

The gambler leapt to his feet and stood glowering at Connor, simulated rage on his face.

'You know right well what I mean, you cheating son of a bitch!'

Connor remained seated, pushing his hand into the pocket of his voluminous ill-fitting suit jacket.

'I ain't packing, Sylvester,' he said as his hand closed over the butt of the snub-nosed .38 in his pocket. 'This is the Sabbath. If you want to shoot it out with me wait till tomorrow and I'll strap on my gun and we can meet on even terms.'

'What even terms did you give Leaker and Fanshawe?' Sylvester snarled. 'You're a back-shooter and a cheat and a liar, and I don't believe you came in here without a gun. Take your hand out of that pocket.'

As he finished speaking Gurney went for the gun strapped to his side. Simultaneously, Sylvia moved in on Connor and he felt a blow in his side as she drove the stiletto into him. Connor grabbed her and swung her round in front of him pulling her into a close embrace and locking her arms so she could not get a second strike. Sylvester had his gun out and fired as Connor made the manoeuvre. Sylvia's body jerked in Connor's arms as the slugs from her brother's gun thudded into her back. She cried out and gaped up at Connor, wide-eyed, opening her mouth as if to say something.

Sylvester was staring in horror as he saw what he had done. Not daring to take the chance of the gun snagging, Connor shot him without removing his pistol from his pocket. The bullet hit him in the guts and he staggered back.

'Noooo!' he screamed and stared down at the wound.

Wild-eyed, he raised his own weapon again and Connor fired once more, this time aiming a little higher and hitting the gambler in the chest. Sylvester staggered back. Sylvia had gone limp in his arms and he allowed her to slip to the floor. She lay there staring up at him, the deadly stiletto still grasped in her hand. On the other side of the table Sylvester was sitting on the floor, his head bowed. A second or two later he toppled over on his side.

Slowly Connor pulled the gun from his pocket and slapped at the smouldering material of his jacket where the muzzle flash had ignited it. He set the gun on the table, knelt down beside the dead woman and gently teased her eyelids shut.

'Sylvia Gurney, may the Lord have mercy on your soul.'

He stood and came round the table to the dead gambler and said the same prayer over him. The patrons of the saloon were crowding round, staring with wide-eyed incredulity at the two bodies. They had witnessed the whole episode from when the gambler had stood and accused Connor of cheating and then the action had been too swift for them to follow.

'The woman has a dagger in her hand,' someone called.

They crowded round, staring in wonder at the long slim blade. As he stood up from his kneeling position Connor put his hand to his side and winced.

'You hurt, sheriff?'

'A knife in the kidneys is all.'

He came back to the woman's body and pointed to the stiletto.

'That's what she used on the prisoners who were murdered. Her partner kicked up some trouble in here and lured Tom out to deal with it. She broke the prisoners out and murdered them. They were supposed to testify against the people who were responsible for ordering the murder of the Amerys.

111

These assassins were hired to silence them and to kill me as well.'

There was a disturbance at the doors and Tom and Jude came in the deputy carrying a shotgun and Jude a rifle. Behind them was Doctor Lytton.

'What the Hell happened?'

'They tried to kill the sheriff,' someone said. 'The woman has a knife long as a bayonet, tried to stick him with it.'

Doctor Cameron came over and knelt by the body of the woman and examined her.

'She's dead. I can't see any wounds.'

'Turn her over. She was shot in the back.'

The doctor moved over and knelt by the second body.

'Dead as a pack rat,' he pronounced. 'You hurt, Sheriff?'

Connor was taking off his suit jacket and pulled up his shirt. As he stripped it could be seen why his clothes fitted him so badly. Strapped around him were panels of leather that had the distinctive look of saddle flaps. As they fell away blood could be seen on Connor's vest.

'This is what saved me. I figured they would both come at me – Sylvia with the poniard and Sylvester with his gun. The leather stopped the blade from going in too far.'

The doctor placed his bag on the table and pulled up the vest to expose a small wound in Connor's side, dark with blood. He busied himself cleaning and dressing the wound. Connor divested himself of the rest of his leather armour and turned to Jude.

'I have you to thank for this outcome. It was your leather underwear and the oversize suit that protected me.'

'Yeah, well, I got me a regular wardrobe of surplus clothes from folk as I have to bury. The fella as owned that suit was quite fussy as to how he was going to look, come Judgment Day. His widow delivered two suits; it was a helluva task to dress him and then await her approval and then she made us try on the other suit afore she made up her mind. As you can see from the size he was a big man and Tom and me were fair exhausted by the time we dressed and undressed him a couple of times. I reckon he weighed over three hundred pounds. The coffin was a big one too. Took eight fellas to carry it.'

'It must have been a big event,' Connor remarked.

Jude grinned at him. The doctor finished bandaging the wound.

'I don't think the blade went in enough to do any damage. You'll be sore for a while. But keep it clean and come by and see me from time to time so as I can change the dressing.'

'Thanks, Doc, what do I owe you?'

'Two dollars. And now I want to get back home and finish my Sunday dinner.'

CHAPTER TWENTY-FIVE

Steve McLeish was stony-faced, staring with narrowed eyes at Hawley, the banker from Bernville.

'He killed them – killed them both?' he said, his voice tight and strained.

'I'm afraid so. Happened two days ago. I came as soon as I could get away.'

The men were in the businessman's study. McLeish placed his hands on the top of the desk and leaned over.

'The bastard! The bastard!'

He shook his head from side to side.

'The Silver Angels, they called themselves. I want the names of the men who helped Connor. I'll ruin every son of a bitch as helped kill them.'

'There weren't anyone else. He did it all on his lonesome.'

McLeish raised his head and stared at the banker.

'That's impossible. No ordinary man could stand against those two and survive.'

'I tell you, I had it from eye witnesses. There was no one else involved.'

'Tell me how it happened.'

'They were in a card game, just Connor and the Gurneys. The sheriff kept winning. Sylvester accused Connor of cheating. Sylvia was sitting by the sheriff and she put a knife into his side. Connor pulled her in front of him as Sylvester opened fire and he hit her instead. The sheriff shot Sylvester.'

'How bad was Connor hurt from Sylvia's knife?'

'Hardly scratched. He had some kind of leather stuff wrapped around him under his clothes as if he knew she would stab him and that saved him.'

'What about the witnesses Connor has in jail? Are they still willing to testify?'

'You needn't worry about those two. They're both dead. Someone busted them out of the jail and knifed them.'

McLeish nodded thoughtfully, his face a grim mask.

'Damn him! Damn him to Hell and back!'

For some moments there was silence as McLeish stared bleakly into the distance.

'Dargan, Seward Dargan,' he said at last.

'Dargan ... surely not.'

'And why not?'

'There are numerous stories of his barbarity. He is wanted in several states for murder and worse. I ... I would not wish him upon Bernville.'

McLeish turned a bleak face to the banker.

'To Hell with what you wish or no. This son of a bitch has proved more tenacious than I would ever have believed. He needs to be taken care of and Dargan is the only man I can think of to do the job. Whatever other damage he inflicts on the populace of Bernville they deserve it for electing that do-gooder as sheriff. Don't worry about Dargan. I will be able to control him. I will pay him well so he obeys me. Don't fret. Whatever happens in Bernville I will make sure you'll be kept safe.'

Hawley opened his mouth as if to say something more but the look in the businessman's face compelled him to stay silent.

'He'll ride into Bernville and come to you at the bank asking for a job as a security guard. That'll give him a legitimate reason for being in town and also an excuse for any arms he might want to sport.'

'A security guard! Hell, he's wanted for armed robbery in half a dozen states. It'll be like hiring a wolf to guard the lambs during the lambing season.'

'Hawley, trust me. I know what I'm doing. Now let's have a drink to celebrate the sudden demise of Jason blasted Connor.'

The banker raised his glass and drank but he could not suppress the feeling of dread that welled up deep within him.

The stagecoach pulled up outside the Mammoth Hotel and four men and a woman disembarked. They looked ordinary enough citizens visiting Bernville. There was absolutely nothing to indicate they were members of a vicious criminal gang. Between them they were responsible for numerous robberies and murders across the western states of America. Their leader, Seward Dargan, and his second-in-command,

Andrew Laurence, rode into town on horseback and pulled up at the bank. Dargan pushed his hat back on his head and grinned across at Laurence.

'Who would have believed it – me and you as bank security guards?'

'Sweet – sweet as Kentucky whiskey.'

'Let's go in and introduce ourselves.'

They swung down and tied up the horses before sauntering inside the bank.

'George Brown and Leslie Jones,' Dargan told the clerk, 'We got an appointment with Mr Hawley.'

In a short while they were ushered into the bank manager's office. Hawley exhibited signs of nervousness as he told his visitors to sit. From behind his desk Hawley appraised the outlaws imposed on him by McLeish.

Dargan he considered to be almost handsome with his square jaw and lean build. He had a well-trimmed moustache. His companion had a Mongolian cast to his features with his tight eyes giving him a mean look. He had a goatee and moustache, also well manicured.

'Howdy,' Dargan greeted Hawley amicably. 'We come for that guard job. We're well experienced in bank security.'

'So I've been advised. When can you start?'

'I guess in the morning will do. Before that we'll familiarize ourselves with the town and get to know the opposition. Tell us what you know of this Jason Connor.'

'He's dangerous as a puma. Twice, McLeish sent people against him and each time they came off second best. I advise you not to underestimate him.'

'Who did he take out?'

'Seth Leaker and Pete Fanshawe were the first. Fanshawe was sheriff and he gathered a posse to arrest Connor. Connor shot them all to Hell. Before that Connor had killed Leaker

116

in a shootout and Fanshawe thought to use that as an excuse to arrest Connor. When the gun smoke cleared Connor ended up with the sheriff's job. Then a couple who called themselves the Silver Angels came into town to take him out. They also ended up dead.'

Dargan pursed his lips and nodded thoughtfully.

'I know the Silver Angels – Sylvia and Sylvester. He did well to survive against them. Has this Connor any special friends or associates. Always good to know where a fella's weak points are.'

'Hard to tell. He is championing a widow woman name of Amery, but I don't know if he has his sights set on her. He arrived here with her nephew, an orphan boy who he seems to have befriended. Other than that as far as I know he has no connection with the town.'

'I guess we'd better go and introduce ourselves to this fearsome lawman.'

The visitors got to their feet.

'McLeish paid us half for this job and you were to pay the balance when we completed the task. How soon will we be able to get our hands on the money once we are finished?'

'I can pay you when you have fulfilled your part of the bargain. I have more than sufficient funds to pay you.'

'That's all I need to know. We'll be seeing you.'

Outside in the street Dargan turned to Laurence.

''You hear that. The money's in the bank. You heard what the sonabitch said. I have more than sufficient funds to pay you.'

The outlaws grinned at each other.

'Seeing as this Connor is so formidable I do believe we must be due a bonus when we kill him.'

'Sure thing. I guess emptying the bank vaults should be a piece of apple pie seeing as we have a working relationship with the bank security.'

Grinning hugely, the two bandits lead their mounts down the street towards the sheriff's office.

CHAPTER TWENTY-SIX

Connor looked up as the door opened and the two strangers entered. He noted the low-slung guns and knew instinctively these were dangerous men. After the assassination attempt by the Gurneys he took precautions not to be caught napping. He kept his hand close to the .45 he had placed under the desk.

'Howdy, fellas, what can I do for you?'

'We just arrived in town, Sheriff and want to introduce ourselves seeing as we are in the same business so to speak. We're security guards employed at the bank. This is Leslie Jones and I'm George Brown.'

'Nice to see Mr Hawley takes his security so seriously. Though as far as I know the bank's never been attacked. From what I know Hawley has a vault that is said to be impregnable.'

'There's rumours a dangerous gang is heading this way. I don't know how reliable the report is. But I'm sure Andy and I can handle it. Though if we need help I hear tell you're a right handy fella with a gun.'

'Just average, but now that you've warned me I'll keep an eye out for anything suspicious.'

'Sure is reassuring, a man with your reputation being on our side, Sheriff.'

After the pair left Connor sat staring at the door with a

thoughtful frown on his face.

'George Brown and Leslie Jones,' he mused. 'Now why would he then call his buddy Andy?'

He pulled out a sheaf of wanted posters and began leafing through them. It was some time later when he leaned back in his chair and examined one particular poster.

'By the Lord God Almighty, does Hawley know who he's dealing with? One of the most dangerous felons the West has ever spawned.'

For long moments he sat there thinking of this new danger, then he got up and, after carefully scrutinizing the street, he stepped out on the boardwalk and made his way down to the livery, where he found Jude and told him what he had learned of the men who had been hired by Hawley to guard the bank.

'By Jehoshaphat, if this is true we have to warn Hawley. He obviously doesn't know the danger his bank is in, or even that his own life might be in jeopardy.'

'That's debatable. I have my suspicions about Hawley. He sold the note he held on the Amery farm to McLeish. It could only have been him as authorized Leaker to go out to the Amery place and evict Mrs Amery. When I intervened I upended a rotten log that concealed a lot of unsavoury dealings, one of which was the murder of Sidney Amery among other shady transactions. McLeish wants that ranch and he must be in a hurry for him to go to the bother of employing that crew of hellhounds. Sheriff Fanshawe and his buddy Leaker were angels compared to this Dargan fella. Do me a favour and nose around and find out if any more strangers have come into town in the last day or two.'

'As a matter of fact I just rented out a buggy to a fivesome – four men and a woman. Said they were thinking of buying a property here. Asked me directions to the smallholdings and ranches in the area.'

'What direction did they head?' Connor asked, an uneasy feeling growing in him.

'East, I guess, I weren't paying much attention. Just pointed them in that direction.'

'That's out towards the Amery ranch.'

Jude turned and gazed up at Connor.

'What are you thinking?' he asked.

'Dargan and Laurence arrive in town and visit me at the jail just to let me know who they are and that they have me in their sights. While I am worrying about what they are up to and wondering when they intend to hit me, the other members of the gang ride out to the Amery place to reconnoitre the target. I got a bad feeling about all this.'

'You want I should follow the ones as went out to the ranch?' Jude asked.

'Nah! That might only provoke them into doing something rash. I guess I'll just have to sit tight and wait for them to show their hand. Damnit, I feel like a beaver in a trap waiting for the hunter to come and drag me out and relieve me of my pelt. Let me know when that bunch in the buggy gets back.'

Connor wandered back down the street, again feeling decidedly uneasy as he scrutinized the buildings wondering if a sniper was watching his movements. He arrived back at the jail and retired inside to await developments. It was not long before the next act in the drama began. Jude arrived and came inside the office.

'They're back – only not all of them.'

'What?'

'The buggy those strangers hired is back, but only one man driving. He drove down to the bank and he's there now.'

'What the Hell are they up to? I guess I better get on down

there and see what I can find out.'

When Connor arrived at the bank everything seemed normal. There was no sign of the men he was expecting to find there, just a few customers at the counter making transactions. He went to the counter and waited impatiently for a teller to serve him.

'I wonder if it would be possible to see Mr Hawley?' he asked.

'You'll have to wait, Sheriff. Mr Hawley is with clients at the moment. He gave specific instructions he was not to be disturbed.'

Connor thanked the teller and, going across to the door leading into the office, he opened it and walked inside. The men he was seeking were gathered around the bank manager's desk engrossed in some task.

'Not now,' Hawley called testily without looking up. 'I told you I was not to be disturbed.'

'You never told me,' Connor said.

Hawley looked up and his expression, which was harassed, became even more troubled when he saw who the intruder was.

'Sorry, Sheriff, we are in the middle of business here. If you wait outside I will see you as soon as I have finished.'

The three men gathered around Hawley's desk straightened and looked with interest at the intruder.

'Howdy, Sheriff,' Dargan, alias George Brown, greeted Connor. 'Strange you should drop in at this moment. When we finished here we were going to call on you. There's a little job we want you to do for us. One that should be pleasurable for you.'

Connor did not reply but watched warily knowing he was dealing with three highly dangerous men. His hand hovered over his gun butt as he waited to hear details of whatever devilish scheme the men were hatching. Dargan turned back to Hawley.

'Tell the nice sheriff what he has to do.'

Hawley nervously cleared his throat.

'Aw, Mrs Amery has decided to sell up. I am drawing up the transaction right now. Once the paperwork is complete I will get the money from the vault and have it delivered.'

'What are you on about? The last time I saw her Mrs Amery was adamant she wanted to stay on at the ranch.'

'Oh, things change, Sheriff Connor,' Dargan said.

He indicated the fourth man in the office.

'Mr Cameron here represents a consortium that conducted the negotiations with Mrs Amery. The other members of the syndicate are waiting out at the ranch to conclude the business. Actually, I'm glad you came, Sheriff. Mrs Amery specifically asked for you to deliver the money. Said as you were the only person she could trust.'

Connor was staring at the speaker, his mind in turmoil. There was something very wrong here – something very, very wrong. Dargan was smiling at him and Connor felt his apprehension grow.

CHAPTER TWENTY-SEVEN

It was all arranged. The money was in a satchel hanging on Connor's saddle. All he had to do was deliver it to Mrs Amery and the whole episode would be concluded. The ranch would be purchased by the Cattlemen's Oklahoma Conglomerate, which Connor was convinced was a front for McLeish.

However, just then he was unable to dispute the legality or authenticity of the transaction.

Hawley had shown him the bill of sale signed by Ellen Amery and compared it with her signature on other legal documents in his possession. There was no doubting it was Ellen's signature but Connor was convinced it had been gained under duress. It worried him that the other members of the so-called conglomerate were still out at the ranch and he surmised it was to keep the Amery family secure till the deal was concluded.

Already he had figured out his own role in the business. He would be murdered and the money stolen. His body would be spirited away and it would be assumed he had succumbed to temptation and absconded with the money. All loose ends would be tied up and McLeish would have gotten what he wanted. Connor would be dead and Ellen, without anyone to help her, would be rendered destitute. It all seemed very far-fetched but he was convinced that that was how it was going to be played.

The gang would be holding Ellen Amery and the children under guard to keep him in check. Once they had him in their power he would be killed. And if they were not already dead he figured they just might murder Ellen and the children and blame the deed on him. All the loose ends would be neatly tied up, with no witnesses to contradict their version of events.

He arrived at the copse of trees and saw in the distance the ranch, and stopped. Sliding down from the horse he walked deep inside the trees and tossed the satchel into a stubby oak. It took a couple of throws before it lodged in the branches. He walked back to his mount and stood for a moment gazing back towards the town. Then he mounted and reaching down patted the horse.

'Perhaps today I might go to meet my Maker, but I shall not go alone. I shall have company.'

The horse whickered and shook its head, causing its bridle to rattle.

'Yeah, well, don't worry. I'm sure someone will take care of you and feed you the occasional pail of oats.'

Once the terms of the delivery had been agreed, Connor had walked back to the livery to collect his horse and tell Jude what was happening.

'You can't do this, Jason. They're luring you out there in order to murder you.'

'Yeah, that's how I figure it. But they have the Amery family out there. Somehow they frightened Ellen into signing that bill of sale. I reckon they persuaded her by threatening the children. I have to go along with them for the time being.'

Jude pointed to the satchel Connor was carrying.

'Is that the greenbacks?'

Connor hefted the bag.

'Five thousand dollars.'

Jude whistled.

'I might try for it myself.'

'It is a fraction of what the ranch is worth,' Connor said. 'McLeish is more or less stealing the ranch from Ellen and the children. Plus the fact I doubt if she will ever get this money.'

The hunchback's eyes narrowed and he stared speculatively at Connor.

'Come in the office. There's something I want to show you.'

Jude opened a drawer and took out a small gun wrapped in rawhide thongs, a tobacco tin and a stiletto. He turned and smiled at Connor.

'I took these off the bodies of the dead Gurneys.

Wondered if they might be of any use to you?'

Connor reached out and took the gun.

'By all that's holy, a derringer and harness to secure it.'

'It was strapped to Sylvester's arm, all ready to be shook out when the need arose.'

Jude picked up the tobacco tin and pressed the end causing a blade to shoot out.

'Sharing a smoke with that snake may well have been a mite unhealthy,' the livery owner remarked. 'I thought seeing as you are bent on this suicide mission, these little toys might just give you an edge.'

Now with only those 'toys', as Jude had called them, to aid him, he was riding to what might be certain death. As he got to the gate he saw there was someone sitting on the veranda. Connor noted the revolver in his hand resting on his lap. He noticed the open windows and figured other members of the gang were lurking within the house also with weapons aimed at him.

'Howdy.'

'You bring the money for the sale?'

'Yep.'

'Let's see it.'

The man raised his weapon and pointed it at Connor.

'And don't do anything stupid. We've heard of your reputation. Just hand over the money for the sale and we'll ride outta here.'

'I want to make sure the family is safe.'

'Just drop the money afore I drop you where you sit.'

Connor held his hands well out from his body.

'I sort of figured you were going to act ornery like this so I hid the money back there in the trees.'

He turned and gestured towards the trees just visible in the distance.

'You son of a bitch, why'd you do a dumb thing like that. I've a good mind to shoot you just for the Hell of it.'

'Money's there waiting to be picked up just as soon as I see that Mrs Amery and her kids are safe.'

The gunman stared hard at Connor and he feared he would carry out his threat and shoot him out of hand.

'Get down and shuck any guns you are carrying. I'll take you inside so you can see for yourself.'

Connor dismounted and walked towards the house, at the same time pulling out his gun. Almost immediately a shot blasted out and buried itself in the dirt in front of Connor.

'What the Hell!' he yelled. 'I'm doing as you asked. I was about to ditch my gun.'

'I don't trust you. We know your reputation. Now toss the gun down.'

Connor bent and laid the weapon in the dirt, then continued walking. As he reached the veranda another man stepped out.

'Hold your arms out so I can frisk you. Keep your gun on the son of a bitch.'

The second man patted him down, then roughly pushed him against the wall.

'You as much as make a wrong move and we'll blast you to Hell.'

'Look, I just want to make sure the people who live here are safe. It's my job to protect the citizens of this town. I wouldn't be doing my duty if I let you ride away and then I find a houseful of dead people inside. You say you know my reputation. Well, I know the reputation of the Dargan gang. You're wanted for murder in five states. You say you don't trust me. Well, it works both ways. I don't trust you.'

'Who told you we were Dargan's mob? We're legit traders come to make a land deal.'

Connor was pushed roughly towards the door.

'Get in there. Make any moves that look a mite suspicious and you'll be dead and the people you are so protective of will be dead, also.'

CHAPTER TWENTY-EIGHT

As Connor came through the door he saw Ellen sitting in a chair in the middle of the room. Another member of the gang stood by her with a gun held at her head. Anger was growing in him as he noticed the bruising on her face and the blood caked on her nose. By the window a woman stood watching him. She was of slight build with black curly hair and pale features and had a Colt pushed into the sash on her waist. Connor knew from reading her poster this was Muriel Sykes, a viper capable of luring men to their doom. Muriel Sykes was dangerous as were all the members of the Dargan gang. Ellen stared at him with a mute appeal in her eyes.

'Howdy, Ellen, I see they have been treating you a mite rough.'

He glanced sideways at his captors.

'It took four of you to beat this female into submission?'

'Shut the Hell damn it up!' snarled the man holding the gun to Ellen's head. 'What about the money?'

'Like I told your friend here, when I am sure the family is safe I'll bring in the money. Where are the kids?'

'They're upstairs. They ain't been harmed.'

'I need to see for myself.'

'Jed, you take him up. And remember any funny tricks

and those kids will be orphans.'

'"Charity that is pure and undefiled is to visit orphans and widows in their affliction, and to keep oneself unstained from the world",' Connor quoted. '"Repent now you sinners before the wrath of the Lord fall upon you."'

'Preacher man, I ain't got no truck with stuff like that, so keep it to yourself. Now hurry it up afore my patience runs out.'

A surly youth with mean eyes jabbed his pistol in Connor's stomach.

'Upstairs. If it was me I'd just gut shoot you and leave you to bleed to death.'

'"The Lord tests the righteous, but his soul hates the wicked and the one who loves violence."'

'Shut up,' was the reply, said with such vehemence that spittle sprayed into Connor's face.

With the gunman following, Connor went up the stairs.

'Alexander, Emma, it's Jason. Are you all right?'

'Jason, have you come to rescue us? We're locked in.'

'Where's Ma? What have they done to her?'

'Your mother is all right. You'll all be fine.'

He turned to the surly youth.

'Where's the key?'

'No key. You heard them. They're all right.'

'Before I go I want to pray for them. Children, I want you to sing a hymn as loud as you can. Big, big voices.'

Connor began to sing.

'How many are my foes, Lord!
How many rise against me!'

By the third line of the psalm the children had joined in.

'Louder,' Connor yelled and then massaged his throat.

'Damnit, I need a smoke,' he complained and pulled out his tobacco tin.

'Care to join me.'

Connor saw indecision in the youth's eyes and it was then he depressed the lid and the blade clicked out. Two things happened then. He grabbed for the gun, jamming his fingers in the trigger guard and at the same time driving the blade into the gunman's throat. Blood spurted out as he slammed the man against the wall. He could feel the body convulsing and held him upright as he trashed about in his death throes. He joined in the singing, roaring out the lines trying to cover up any noises the dying man was making.

How many say of me,
God will not save that one.'

The body went slack and Connor lowered it to the floor. He recovered the gun and stuffed it in his holster. His hand was covered in blood and he wiped it on the dead man's jacket. He went to the stairs and walked down stepping into the room where three pairs of eyes watched his every movement the woman over by the door now and the man by the window.

'You will shatter the jaws of my foes
You will break the teeth of the wicked.'

Connor held his hands out as if in a benediction and the derringer slid into his hand. He shot the man guarding Ellen in the face and he staggered back, his gun slipping from his hand. Then Connor was pulling his new gun and ducked instinctively as the gunman by the window fired at him. Connor turned to fire at the man. He felt a blow on his arm as the woman pulled her gun and shot at him. He staggered sideways and that probably saved him from the shots fired at him by the gunman at the window.

Recovering his balance, Connor fired two slugs into the bandit and saw him crash back into the window. The window frame gave way under the impact and the man went through, coming to rest half inside the room. The woman was still firing at him and a bullet stung his neck.

'Drop it!' he yelled at her.

She bared her teeth in a snarl and turned her gun on Ellen and pulled the trigger. Before a shocked Connor could react she had fled out the door. Ellen slumped in the chair and keeled over sliding to the floor. Quickly Connor ran across to her.

'Ellen! Oh, my God, Ellen!'

There was a mess of blood on her blouse. She was staring up at him, a shocked look on her face. Desperately he looked around for something to staunch the bleeding and ran into the kitchen. He snatched up towels and came back to her side and began packing the wound.

'I'm so sorry, Ellen. I tried to keep you and your family safe and I've failed.'

She tried to smile and then closed her eyes.

'You're a good man, Jason,' she whispered. 'Are the children safe?'

'Yes, they're still up there in their room. I'll bring them down as soon as I've got you comfortable.'

He gathered cushions and placed them under her head.

'Don't try to move. I'll get the children.'

Quickly he went upstairs and tried the door of the bedroom and found it locked.

'It's Jason,' he called. 'Stand back, I'll have to break the door.'

One solid kick and the door burst open. The children ran to him and he held them.

'You need to be brave. Your mother has been hurt. Bring blankets. We need to wrap her up and keep her warm.'

'You're bleeding!' Emma exclaimed pointing to Connor's neck

He could feel the stickiness of the drying blood against

his shirt collar.

'And your arm,' Alexander cried out.

'It's okay. It's only a scratch. Now go look after your mother.'

They did as they were told and went downstairs with the blankets. When they had done all they could to make Ellen comfortable, Connor dragged the body of the gunman out into the yard and pushed his dead companion through the window where it was leaning half inside and half outside. It was awkward work as he felt the wound in his arm stiffening. His horse was gone and he figured the woman was riding to inform Dargan of developments. He needed to work fast.

'Get a drink for your mother and yourselves. I'll go into town and fetch the doc. She needs urgent medical care. Keep her warm and keep yourselves safe. You have been very brave. I don't know anyone that would have held up so well.'

He saddled up a horse, finding it a chore with his wounded arm and began the ride back to town, blaming himself bitterly for how he had failed the Amery family. As he pounded into the livery he was calling for the owner.

'Jude! Jude! Where in the goddamn Hell are you?'

The hunchback appeared from the back.

'Jason, what the hell's going on? My God, you've been shot!'

'Harness up a rig while I go and fetch Doc Lytton. Mrs Amery has been shot.'

Dismounting, Connor left the livery at a run before Jude could question him. In a very short time he had rounded up the doc and told him what needed doing.

'What about that arm and your neck?' Doc Lytton asked.'

'It'll do for now. Mrs Amery is the one in need. You get out there as fast as you can. She's in a bad way.'

'I ain't budging till I bind up that arm and your neck

is covered in blood, too. Good God man, you're all shot to pieces!'

In spite of Connor's protests the doc refused to shift till he had cleansed and dressed his wounds. When they arrived back at the livery Jude was in the driving seat of a fast-looking rig.

'Aren't you coming?' Jude asked as Connor handed the doc up into the passenger seat and stepped back.

'No, I got some more business to attend in town.'

While watching the buggy drive out of town Connor checked his hardware, punching fresh shells into his pistols and reloading the derringer. At last satisfied he was ready, he stalked down the street.

CHAPTER TWENTY-NINE

Connor kept to the boardwalk, his gaze sweeping over buildings and alleyways on the lookout for an ambush. Curious townsfolk looked askance at their sheriff, and one or two called out a greeting but he ignored them. Nothing occurred to cause him any alarm and he kept going steadily till he reached the bank. It was only then he drew his pistol, took a deep breath and stepped inside.

He gazed around at the empty room. There was no one at the counter. He paused by the door before walking quietly forward. Something prompted him to look behind the counter and he noticed bloodstains on the floor; on the wall there were ominous splashes of red.

Cautiously he stepped towards the office door behind

which earlier that day he had agreed to deliver five thousand dollars to the Amery ranch. Since then three men had died and Ellen Amery lay seriously wounded. He tried the door but it was locked. Keeping to one side he used his pistol to tap on the glass that had Hawley's name painted on. There was no response.

'Hello,' he called. 'Hawley, are you there?'

He had a bad feeling about this and without any more ado he stove in the glass panel with the barrel of his gun and called out again. Getting no response he peered through the broken glass. He could see a body lying on the floor. He reached inside and unfastened the door.

The two clerks he had seen earlier out front were sprawled on the office floor. Their throats had been cut and their blood soaked the carpet. The vault door was ajar and he pulled it wide. Inside, the bank manager was gagged and trussed securely. Connor holstered his gun and stepped inside the vault and undid the gag.

'Thank God you're here, Sheriff. I was getting desperate. They killed poor Benton and Wilkes. I was sure they were going to do the same to me.'

He held out his hands expecting Connor to untie the ropes. Instead the sheriff squatted down and thoughtfully regarded the banker. Ignoring the proffered bonds Connor took out the makings and began building a smoke.

'Sheriff, would you get these ropes of me?'

'How you are fallen from Heaven, O Day Star, son of Dawn! How you are cut down to the ground, you who laid the nations low!'

'What?'

'For the wages of sin is death. Mrs Amery is lying at death's door, shot by your female associate Muriel Sykes. Your clerks are out there with their throats cut and here you are in your empty vault trussed up like a turkey dinner. What say you now about dealing with killers and thieves like Dargan and McLeish?'

'Please, I was not aware of the nature of those people. I hired them in all good faith.'

Connor stood and stepped out of the vault.

'Where are you going? Release me.'

Connor ignored the banker's pleading and sat down at the desk. He pulled pen and paper from a drawer and began writing.

'Damn you! I demand you release me at once.'

'The greedy bring ruin to their households, but the one who hates bribes will live. I am writing down the sordid tale of a corrupt banker and his evil taskmaster and their dishonest dealings. I want you to sign it.'

Connor cut the ropes on the banker's wrists, and held out the paper and pen.

'I had no knowledge of their plan. I tell you I didn't know what they were up to. I'm as much a victim as everyone else.'

Connor set the paper down and pulled out a pair of cuffs and fastened them on the banker.

'What are you doing?'

'Keeping you safe.'

Connor got to his feet and stepped out of the vault.

'I'm gonna shut this door. I don't know the combination so you will stay there till you expire from lack of air or starvation. It don't matter which. When they get the safe open they'll guess Dargan locked you in there. They'll find that confession and reckon you were trying to get your revenge on the people who left you to die.'

'No, wait! If I sign that I'll be signing my own death warrant. Do you want that on your conscience?'

'For we must all appear before the judgment seat of Christ,

so that each one may receive what is due for what he has done in the body, whether good or evil.'

As he finished speaking Connor began to close the vault.

'Wait, wait! I'll sign!'

Connor dragged the banker out and set him at the desk with the pen and paper.

'There now, that wasn't too hard. Hawley, I'm arresting you for conspiring to rob a family of their property, murder and attempted murder.'

'You can't arrest me. I got to get as far away as possible from McLeish.'

Connor sawed the ropes around the banker's ankles.

'On your feet. We're walking down the jail.'

Hawley opened his mouth to say something but the look in Connor's face stopped him. With drooping shoulders and stumbling pace he headed from the bank down the street towards the jail where Connor locked him in a cell.

'They'll kill me now, for sure,' the banker protested.

'Don't worry; I'll keep you alive till the trial. After all, you're my star witness.'

'There won't be any trial. Both you and I will both be dead before long. McLeish will send Dargan back here with orders to kill us both.'

'Have you forgotten? Dargan tried to kill me once already and lost half his gang in the attempt.'

It was late in the day when the buggy arrived back from the ranch. When Connor saw the children in the carriage he knew something bad had happened. Doc Lytton shook his head.

'I could do nothing. The poor woman was too far gone.'

The children sat in the buggy red-eyed from weeping and looking at Connor as if he was their only contact with the real world.

'I'm sorry, children. It was all my fault. If I hadn't interfered and just given them the money, they might have ridden off and your ma would still be alive.'

Alexander was shaking his head.

'We heard them. They were going to kill you and then take us with them and sell us.'

'And they were dead in their trespasses and sins. There seems no depth to the perfidy of men.'

Connor sighed deeply.

'What are we going to do with you? You will need somewhere safe to stay till this dreadful business is over. Emma, is there any of your family we can get in touch with?'

The young girl shook her head, too filled with grief to speak.

'I got room at my place,' Jude said. 'They're welcome to stay till something can be arranged.'

The hunchback looked quizzically at the children.

'Mind you, they'll have to look after themselves. I ain't much of a hand at housekeeping or cooking, much less looking after children.'

'What do you say, kids?' Connor asked.

They nodded dumbly, too numb and miserable to think about anything, only the terrible events of the past days that had torn their lives asunder.

CHAPTER THIRTY

Connor was out at the ranch overseeing that everything was in order. He had hired Ben Durian, a cowboy of indeterminate age who had drifted into town and had been asking around for work. Not wanting to let him think he was being hoodwinked, Connor told Durian the story of the ranch.

'The people who want this place are desperate and ruthless. As a direct result of their attempts to take possession there have been several killings in recent weeks, including the murder of the man and woman who owned the place. So if you see any suspicious-looking strangers, don't hang about – vamoose! Whatever you do, don't confront them. Come straight into town and tell me. I don't want any more innocents massacred.'

Ben pulled out a sack of Bull Durham and began building a smoke.

'Sheriff, I ain't one to run from trouble. I've been involved in range wars and I know how dirty they can get. I never ran from no man and I don't aim to start now.'

For long moments the two men eyed each other. Connor sensed this was a man who had no sign of yellow in his make-up. Ben struck a match and lit his smoke.

'I ain't telling you to run. I'm ordering you to get the Hell outta here at the first hint of trouble. You're no good to me crippled or killed by the gang of butchers we're dealing with. You hear me!'

Suddenly the cowboy smiled, immediately lightening up his dour countenance.

'Okay, boss. Just like to know where I stand.'

He lit his cigarette and offered the tobacco sack to Connor, who took it and began fashioning his own rollup. They smoked in silence for a while.

'I ain't no angel, Sheriff,' the cowboy said eventually. 'I been in prison a time or two and I've killed, also. But I've come out here looking to start afresh. '

'For all men have sinned and fall short of the glory of God,' Connor said, and blew a plume of smoke into the air.

'Though your sins are like scarlet, they shall be white as snow. Though they are red with the blood of men they shall be washed clean.'

'Another thing, Reverend, I ain't much on church-going. Never could see much in all that holy malarkey stuff.'

'A good man is known by his deeds, not by his avowal before the world.'

'Yeah, I guess you have the Good Book learnt off by heart and could quote me plenty. It don't coil no lariat for me.'

They both looked up at the sound of hoof beats. Coming across the plain was a body of horsemen.

'Now who in the devil's name are they?' Connor puzzled.

He reached down and unhooked the loop holding his gun secure in his holster then turned to his companion and was surprised to see a six-gun in the man's hand.

'Seward Dargan is a friend of mine. When he took on the job of bounty hunter he asked me to suss out the lay of the land. I guess I get to claim a share in the reward money on your head, Mr Preacher Man.'

'Their throat is an open grave and with their tongues they keep deceiving for the poison of asps is under their tongues,' Connor said, a tinge of resignation in his voice.

The riders pulled up at the ranch with Dargan in the lead. He smiled at the pair in the yard.

'I see you caught the killer, Ben.'

'Shall we hang him now? Send him to this God of his he's so fond of preaching about.'

'Nah, McLeish says it has all got to be done lawfully. We take him back to town and after a trial we'll hang him all proper and legal.'

Dargan climbed down from his horse and walked across to Connor.

'Keep your guns on this lobo. He's as dangerous as a nest

of rattlers. Marty, bring up some rawhide. We got to tie this maverick on his horse so he doesn't pull any more stunts. He has a bad habit of killing off my friends.'

'I could claim the same about you. Killing Ellen Amery was a vile act and one for which you must pay.'

Dargan took Connor's gun and tucked it in his belt.

'I don't know what you're talking about. I didn't kill any woman.'

'No, but that she-cat you sent out here did. So I hold you responsible.'

'You're not in any position to hold anything. On the ride back to town just say your prayers.'

An outlaw with a thick moustache drooping over his lips approached carrying strands of rawhide. Once he was secure Dargan searched Connor for further weapons and found the derringer.

'Muriel told me about your hideout gun. Shot Tom Burns with it. Muriel was fond of Tom so she shot your woman to even things up.'

'You are the Devil's brood. You are men who love darkness rather than the light because your evil deeds cannot bear the scrutiny of daylight.'

Dargan turned away from his prisoner.

'Let's get back to town. I can't wait to fit this preacher fella with a rope necktie.'

The ride back to town was made in silence. Connor surreptitiously observed the individual members of the gang, speculating on their strengths and weaknesses, but they all looked as hard and capable as the man he had hired as a ranch-hand, Ben Durian.

'"I have fallen amongst lions whose teeth are spears and arrows and their tongues sharp swords."'

'What the Hell you on about?' growled one of the outlaws

in his escort.

'I was praying that you might repent of your sins before I kill you,' replied the prisoner.

When they got to town the gang headed straight for the jail.

'Bring him inside,' ordered Dargan. 'We've a nice cosy cell for him.'

Connor wondered if this was the time to make his move before he was locked inside his own jail. It was as if Dargan had read his mind. There was a flurry of movement around him as the gang members unlimbered their guns and trained them on him.

'A hint of anything amiss and you have my permission to gun him down,' the gang boss said.

Inside, sitting behind Connor's desk was a big, strong-looking man in a broadcloth suit tailored to fit his wide frame. Hawley had been freed from his cell and was sat on the other side of the stranger.

'Glad you could make it,' the banker said with a thin smile. 'This is Mr McLeish, the man whose plans for the development of Bernville you've been obstructing. But not for much longer.'

CHAPTER THIRTY-ONE

Connor lay at full stretch on the bunk, his hands behind his head, and stared placidly at the ceiling. His meeting with McLeish had been brief.

'So you're the fella that's been standing in the path of

progress,' the businessman stated. 'Some people have no vision. I would have been prepared to offer you a position in my organization but you choose to oppose me at every turn. Now you'll pay the penalty for your stubborn short-sightedness.'

'The slaughter of the innocents seems to be an essential part of this progress you boast about. That was the bit that stuck in my craw. A man who uses murderers and outlaws as the tools of his trade is no better than those who carry out his orders. I am not a killer for hire.'

'For a man who claims not to be a killer you seem to have done your fair share. However, your days of killing are over. I have sent for a magistrate and you will be tried in a court of justice. It will all be above board and legal. At the end of the trial you will be hanged for all the crimes you have committed. In the meantime, you are relieved of your duties as sheriff and Durian will act in your place till a man we can trust to keep law and order in this town can be elected. Take him away.'

Before he could make reply Connor was bundled off to the cells. Now he lay and contemplated his fate. He had no doubt McLeish had a crooked judge on his payroll. The trial would be a farce and at the end of it he would be taken out and hanged. Contrary to fretting about his own fate he was speculating on what would happen to Alexander and Emma.

For the time being they were safe living with Jude, but if any legal difficulties arose regarding the ownership of the ranch, Connor feared that they would either be disposed off or bullied into signing away their rights. They would be left destitute, with no one to protect them. And then the gate to the outer office rattled and one of Dargan's deputies ushered in the very people he had been thinking about. Connor sat up.

'Jason!' Alexander exclaimed.

A woman appeared behind the children as they scurried to the bars of the cell and peered in at the prisoner.

'Looks like you still got some friends left,' the guard sneered, ogling the woman.

She ignored him and came over to join the children smiling uncertainly in at him.

'I don't know if you remember me, Mr Connor. I'm Catherine Webb. My father owns the dry goods store.'

'How do you do, ma'am? I remember seeing you in the store.'

'Jude asked me to help him look after the children. They wanted to come and see you. I brought you some food.'

She indicated her basket draped with a cloth and then turned to the deputy.

'If you could open the cell door I can pass this to Mr Connor?'

'We already had a look inside.' The deputy sniggered. 'There ain't nothing in the basket to help you escape. I have to ask permission to open the cell.'

He turned and yelled the request through the open door. There came a muffled reply and he poked his head outside. To Connor's amazement Catherine pulled up her skirts exposing her underwear and pulled out a cotton wrapped bundle. She thrust this through the bars and recovering from his surprise at the unexpected vision of female lingerie, Connor tossed the bundle under the bunk. When the guard turned back to the room the little group by the cell were waiting expectantly.

'Seb is coming in to help.'

He pulled his gun. Seb arrived carrying a shotgun which he aimed into the cell.

'We've been told you're a mighty dangerous *hombre*. No need to tell you any trouble and you'll be filled with lead.'

The deputy moved forward.

'Move back from the door,' he ordered.

Connor stepped back. Unlocking the door the deputy motioned Catherine to slide the basket inside. Keeping his gun trained on Connor he locked up again.

'Enjoy your dinner. It might be your last. The judge arrives on tonight's stage. We might get to hang you tomorrow.'

'You have no right to hang Jason,' Alexander blurted. 'He ain't done nothing wrong.'

'It's all right,' Connor said. 'Don't waste your breath on these fellas. They're bandits and killers employed by the biggest crook in the county.'

'Who're you calling crooks? You're the one locked up.'

Connor did not deign to reply but turned his attention to the people who had come to visit and by the weight of the package they had delivered, a means of escaping the fate his jailors were sure he was due.

'You kids behaving yourselves,' he asked, 'and not giving Jude too much trouble?'

The children nodded dumbly and he could see the fear in their eyes.

'They've been very well behaved,' Catherine answered for them. 'I think they are very worried about you.'

'Hey, fellas, don't you be concerned about me. That old judge will declare me innocent and release me. Then he'll give me my job back again. Is Jude looking after you?'

'Yes, he's very kind,' Alexander answered.

Emma reached out and took Catherine's hand.

'Miss Catherine helps. She is very good to us.'

'And she's a good cook,' Alexander added.

Connor looked up at the woman and she blushed under his gaze.

'I do what I can to help out.'

'"Wherefore by their fruits ye shall know them. The good that you do is a sign of your kind heart. Minister to my children and so shall it be given back to ye sevenfold."'

'Time up!' a harsh voice broke in.

As they were hustled from the jail the children called out their goodbyes and kept waving till Connor could see them no more. The outer door slammed and the key turned in the lock.

'At least they are safe for the time being,' he muttered. 'Now let's see what they brought me.'

He took the basket to the bunk and pulled back the cover and peeked inside. Then he bent and recovered the bundle Catherine had smuggled in under her skirts. He looked with some satisfaction at the five-shot Cooper pocket revolver with five-inch barrel.

'This will do very nicely for afters.'

He slid the revolver inside his shirt and practised pulling it out till he was fairly certain it would be available when the time arose to use it. Only then did he turn his attention to the basket.

'Fried potatoes, fried chicken and apple pie. Bless their kind hearts.'

Without more ado Connor spread the cotton cloth the gun had been wrapped in and set out his dinner on top of it.

CHAPTER THIRTY-TWO

Three of the Dargan gang appeared inside the jail. The one with the droopy moustache was jangling the bunch of keys as he walked over to Connor's cell. The other two placed themselves one each side and kept their guns on the prisoner.

'Time for the final act, Connor. The trial is all arranged, though why McLeish is bothering with such a farce baffles me. I'd just as well take you out and hang you without all this palaver. Must have cost him a packet to buy that judge.'

He held up a set of handcuffs and smirked.

'You'll need these. We got leg irons for you as well.'

Connor stood up from the bunk.

'I've been praying for you,' he said. 'I want you to repent of your sinful ways before it is too late.'

His jailer sniggered and his companions joined in.

'We're touched. What would you have us do? Give up our life of banditry and high living and push cows instead. Nah, preacher, I tried that. All it gets you is a life of hard labour and chicken-feed wages at the end of it. Hold out your hands while I put these irons on. And I warn you we have orders to shoot you at the slightest sign of trouble. If you want to commit suicide and cheat the hangman, then you just try and jump us.'

'Do violence to no man, neither accuse anyone falsely and be content with your wages,' Connor advised as he moved towards the door.

He held his left hand out as if offering it for the shackles.

'Yeah, yeah,' the jailor said indifferently.

He reached for the proffered hand and it was at that point Connor pulled his hideout gun and jammed it in the jailor's guts.

'Tell your friends to throw down their weapons or you are in imminent danger of being hurled into the shadowy depths of hell.'

'Hell I will!'

The jailer lashed out at Connor with the cuffs catching

him in the side of the face. Connor instinctively pulled the trigger and his attacker yelled out and would have staggered back only Connor held him upright.

'Drop your weapons or you all die!' he yelled.

The wounded bandit sagged in his grip and his companions took the opportunity to chance a shot at the prisoner. Connor ducked and at the same time fired at the man nearest the door. The stricken man spun away and crashed against the wall. His companion kept on firing and Connor felt a stinging blow across his shoulder. He let go the gut-shot jailer and, with a clear line of fire, shot the third gunman in the chest, throwing him back with the force of the bullets. The man sagged against the wall, trying to bring up his gun but only succeeding in putting another shot into the jailer who was now kneeling in front of Connor and holding onto the bloody hole in his belly.

Connor stepped out of the cell and kicked away the man's weapon. He turned his attention to the other wounded bandit but he was cursing quietly, holding both hands to the wound in his chest. Quickly Connor collected up all the weapons along with the bunch of keys. He stepped out into the main office and locked the door behind him.

Unhurriedly he walked across to the desk that had been his for a short time. He dumped the weapons on top and, retaining one, walked to the outer door and peered into the street. Except for a few horses tied to hitching rails and a couple of stationary wagons, the street appeared empty of people. Connor assumed they were down at the Golden Egg waiting for the impending trial and the noise inside the saloon probably would have masked the gunshots fired inside the jail, which was a sturdy, brick-built building and would have muffled the explosions. He walked back to the desk and regarded his haul of weapons.

He reloaded the Cooper which had served him so well. Then he picked up a Manhattan six-shot Navy revolver and replaced the loads that had been fired. Next he picked a Remington 1875 New Army six-shot single action revolver and checked the loads. For a moment he gazed thoughtfully at his armoury, then rummaged about till he found a belt and holster, which he draped around his waist.

He pouched the Remington and secreted the Cooper inside his shirt. Lastly, he loaded a Colt Peacemaker and tucked that into his belt. He walked back to the barred door and looked into the cell block. The casualties of the shootout were sprawled on the floor with blood leaking into the floor. He sighed deeply.

'"Give succour to the injured and bind up their wounds lest you yourself are found guilty of transgression." Hang on in there, friends. I will fetch Doc Lytton.'

Cautiously, he peered out the front door and then slipped outside. He made his way through the town striding swiftly with his hat pulled down, keeping his countenance hidden. The streets were deserted. Connor grinned wryly, thinking how surprised the people would be if they realized he was out of jail and walking through the town. At the doctor's house he knocked in vain and suddenly thumped the heel of his hand against his forehead.

Of course, the doctor, just like everyone else, would be queuing up for the only show in town – the trial of ex-sheriff Jason Connor.

He entered the house and gathered bandages and cotton pads and a canvas bag to carry his finds and hurried back to the jail. In his absence nothing had changed. Unlocking the cage he went in and examined the men. One of the bandits was dead and one unconscious; the third man cursed steadily at him.

'Son of a bitch,' he swore even as Connor staunched the wound in his chest and told him to hold a cotton pad over it.

'"He healeth the broken in body and bindeth up their wounds,"' Connor replied. 'As soon as I can, I'll send the doc in to attend you. I guess like everyone else in town he has other things on his mind at the moment.'

He did not bother to lock the cage again thinking the wounded men were too far gone to present a danger. At the front door he took a deep breath.

'I guess I'm ready for my trial. Is not devastation fitting for the wicked and a certainty of punishment justified for the workers of iniquity? May the Lord lend strength to my hand and power to my resolution.'

He stepped outside and began the trek along the street towards the Golden Egg and his destiny.

CHAPTER THIRTY-THREE

Outside the saloon Connor made a final check on his weapons before stepping through the doors. The noise was so catatonic no one noticed him. The bartenders were busily serving up liquor as punters vied for their attention. No wonder no one had heard the shots from the jail.

Connor slid to one side, his back against the wall, and scanned the crowd. He spotted McLeish and Dargan sitting at the far end of the bar. Hawley was there also, and a well-dressed gent wearing a black suit and a neatly tied cravat that matched his thatch of silvery grey hair who, Connor guessed, was the judge brought in to pass the death sentence on him.

He took out the Peacemaker and fired a shot into the floor. There was a momentary pause in the volume of noise as the drinkers turned towards the source of the gunshot and then, as they recognized Connor, the hush deepened and a silence so intense settled in the room that it was almost like another being in the saloon.

'Is Doc Lytton here?' Connor called.

'I'm here. What you want me for?'

'There are a couple of wounded men down at the jail. I went looking for you but when I couldn't find you, I took bandages from your place and patched them as best as I could. But I ain't no sawbones. They need your professional attention.'

'Hell, Connor, they'll have to wait. I figure there may be a need in here for my skills now that you have arrived.'

'I have not come here seeking trouble. I come in peace. It seems to me you people are figuring to railroad me into a hanging. I believe a judge has been summoned to preside over my trial. Would the gentleman in question make himself known?'

While he had been talking Connor noticed the men with McLeish were spreading out from the main group. Deliberately, he raised his revolver and fired a shot over their heads. All movement stopped.

'You fellas just stay where I can see you. I don't want to shoot anyone but I know you men for outlaws and killers. Let me tell you good folk of Bernville; the men sitting at that table with your respected banker Hawley are on wanted notices I found down at the law office. Seward Dargan – wanted in five counties for murder, robbery, and rape. The fella to the right of him is Andrew Laurence, wanted for murder and robbery and torture. They are the people hired by the man you would hand your town over to.'

Connor paused and there was a rustle of agitated mur-murings from the crowded saloon as the occupants took in the implications of the speaker's words. McLeish's table was a stationary tableau with none of the men around it daring to move. All knew the calibre of the man confronting them. The fact that he had been locked up safe in jail and now appeared armed and unescorted sent prickles of fear up the spines of his enemies.

'McLeish ordered the killing of one of your most respected citizens,' Connor went on relentlessly. 'Sidney Amery and his son were murdered. And then his wife was murdered by another of McLeish's hirelings.'

McLeish leapt to his feet.

'What's the matter with you people? This man is a known killer and was under arrest but now, by his own admission, he had broken out of jail and shot up the lawfully appointed dep-uties assigned to guard him. How can you believe anything he says? Since he arrived in your town he has killed several times. Show you are men and stand up to him. I'm placing a bounty on his head of ten thousand dollars. Whoever kills him will live in luxury for the rest of his life.'

There was a sudden flurry of movement and the men in the vicinity of the businessman's table went for their irons.

'"The gates of death have been opened onto thee and ye have stood in the shadows of the doors of death,"' Connor yelled as he dropped to the floor.

An eruption of shoots flared out from McLeish's hirelings and punched into the wall where Connor had been standing. He emptied the Peacemaker at the shooters and, without waiting to see the effects of his shooting, scrambled towards a table.

All around the saloon men were also scrambling to get out to the line of fire, some diving to the floor and others making a rush towards the exits. In the confusion Connor managed to change his position and ended up behind a piano, providing him with more substantial protection against the deadly hail of lead coming his way.

Discarding the empty Peacemaker Connor pulled the Remington and waited a moment, listening to the shooting and the thud of the bullets hammering into the piano. He detected a lull in the shooting and surmising the shooters were pausing to reload, he stood up firing at the gunmen as he rose above the level of the piano.

He noted with satisfaction there were two bodies sprawled on the floor and sprayed the area with more lead. Two more men went down and then, as his gun clicked on empty, there was a rush of men towards his refuge.

Connor felt a sting on his shoulder and another in his left arm. He dropped behind the piano again. Dropping the Remington he pulled the Navy revolver. He managed one shot before a heavy body crashed into him and he found himself wrestling with the attacker.

The fight was too close quarters for guns. Connor punched his assailant in the face and the man lashed out at him. There was a sudden heavy blow on the back of his head and Connor went down, twisting away in an effort to get his gun up. A boot kicked his gun hand and he lost his grip on the weapon.

Suddenly he was surrounded by yelling men and was pulled to his feet and thrust into the open. Someone hit him again with a gun barrel and he went to his knees. Dazed he crouched on all fours shaking his head to clear it. He looked up at the men who had taken him. Dargan and Laurence were standing over him, their revolvers trained on him. The furious face of McLeish appeared alongside them. Someone booted Connor in the side and he crumpled to the floor, stabs of agony slicking through him.

'"Consider mine enemies for they are many,"' he muttered, '"and they hate me with cruel hatred."'

CHAPTER THIRTY-FOUR

'Get him on his feet,' snarled McLeish.

They moved one each side of Connor and pulled him upright. He winced as the wound in his arm was roughly gripped and his ribs hurt where he had been kicked. McLeish pushed his face close to Connor.

'I ain't going to bother with a trial. We'll take you out now and hang you.'

The judge came up to the little group with Hawley the banker trailing.

'Surely that would be unwise,' the judge pleaded. 'You told me the man was a killer and you had evidence of his wrongdoing, but I want no part in lynching him.'

'He's too dangerous to be left alive any longer. This affair ends now, legal or not I'm hanging him. You can sign the death warrant when he's good and dead. Take him out.'

They pushed Connor towards the door and the judge called out after them but no one was taking any notice.

'Get a rope,' someone yelled.

'Take him to the livery. They'll have ropes there.'

People spilled out into the street behind them, anxious not to miss the drama. The little procession advanced along the street, Dargan one side and Laurence on the other, with McLeish and Hawley and Ben Durian trailing.

'The end of the trail, Connor,' Dargan sneered.

'Lord, how long wilt thou look on?' Connor said. 'Rescue me from destruction and save my life from the lions.'

'Pray away, holy man, for your days are numbered.'

As they approached the livery a rifle barrel appeared from a window in the top storey.

'Let him go!'

Connor recognized Jude's voice. Immediately his captors released him and pulling their revolvers shot at the figure in the window. Connor was reaching inside his shirt for his hideout gun when a burly body crashed into him and he fell to the dirt. McLeish's face was close to his and twisted up with hatred.

'You have escaped justice too many times. This is the last time you interfere in my business,' he gritted out and began to batter Connor, targeting his blood-soaked arm.

With one hand inside his shirt where he had tried to bring out his hideout gun and his injured arm being pummelled, Connor was defenceless as he squirmed beneath his attacker. McLeish landed a particularly vicious blow on his wound and Connor cried out with the pain.

As his senses reeled he could hear the shooting still going on as the gunmen tried to take out Jude who was firing at them from the upper story of the livery. The occasional crack of the rifle indicated they hadn't succeeded so far.

Connor struggled desperately, his strength draining as McLeish rained punches on him. His assailant reared up and shouted for a weapon. It was a mistake for the pressure on Connor's arm eased and he pulled his hideout gun.

Too late McLeish saw his mistake and made a grab for the weapon as Connor pulled the trigger. A hole mushroomed in the businessman's throat and he grabbed at his neck, blood spurting between his fingers. Connor twisted in time to see

Dargan bringing his pistol to bear on him. There was a click as the hammer fell on an empty. For a moment the gunman stared down at Connor, then turned to run.

Connor shot Dargan in the side of the head and lined up on Laurence. The killer, realizing what was happening, tried to bring his gun to bear on Connor. Connor fired and missed and then Jude's rifle blasted out and the slug hit the gunman in the elbow.

Yelling in agony, he swapped the gun to the other hand but Connor fired again and this time hit the gunman in the chest. The outlaw staggered back, trying to bring up his gun. Connor shot him again and he went over backwards and crashed to the dirt. Connor turned to sight on the third gunman but Ben Durian was fleeing down the street. When he managed to get to his knees and look around there was no one left to fight.

'Thou hast vanquished mine enemies and rescued me from the wicked.'

With a groan he struggled to his feet and, ignoring his bruised and aching body and the blood soaking his shirt, he staggered back down the street, past the saloon where the gaping townsfolk milled about on the boardwalk. Some of them dodged back inside as they saw the bloody figure approaching. But Connor ignored them and kept on going towards the bank.

He stopped outside and thumbed fresh shells into the Manhattan pistol before weaving his way to the door and pushing inside. He was just in time to see Hawley coming out of the office carrying a bulging bag. When the banker saw Connor he stopped.

'Connor, what a surprise. I see you managed to survive. You are certainly one tough *hombre*.'

He hefted the sack into the air in front of him masking his

other hand. Connor's shot hit the bag ploughing through the contents and punched Hawley in the belly. The banker's eyes opened wide with shock. The sack dropped from slack fingers and with it a gun clattered to the floorboards.

'You ... I ...'

But Hawley did not finish what he wanted to say. His knees buckled and he sank to the floor, rolled over and lay staring up at Connor.

'Damn you ...' he managed before his eyes closed and he was still.

'For out of the serpent's mouth shall come a cockatrice and his venom shall have the stench of death about it.'

Slowly Connor walked over to the sprawled body and nudged the sack with his foot. Dollar bills spilled out. He bent and picked up the gun the banker had dropped and studied it for a moment. It was unusual in that it was a Merwin Hulbert, a beautifully engineered revolver with an interchangeable barrel. In this case it was fitted with the short barrel for easy concealment.

Connor tucked the weapon in his waistband, adding to his collection of revolvers. A couple of chairs stood against one wall and he went over and sat down and waited. Before long a man in a black suit edged inside and scuttled across to the dead banker and bent to gather up the sack with the banknotes. Connor noisily cleared his throat.

'Howdy, Judge,' he said. 'How much did they pay you to take part in this fiasco?'

The judge leapt in the air as if stung by a hornet.

'I ... I don't know what you are talking about. I washed my hands of this affair once I heard talk of lynching. I happened by and saw this poor man lying here and thought I could render some assistance.'

'Judge, if you even are qualified to bear such a title, you

are part of a conspiracy to acquire lands and properties by murder, intimidation and bribery. I am arresting you and you will be held in the town jail till I can inform the proper authorities of your part in this chicanery.'

The judge stood his mouth agape.

'You can't do that,' he blustered. 'You are an escaped prisoner and you yourself have been indicted for murder.'

'Have it your own way, then. You can come peacefully or I can slug you so you will be easier to handle.'

Connor made to move towards the judge.

'Wait … wait a moment. This would ruin me. I wasn't aware of all the facts when I was asked to take on this case. I have influence in Washington. I could be useful to a man like you.'

Connor eyed the judge thoughtfully, then walked across to him. The judge cowered back from the blood-splattered figure.

'Get in that office and bring that money.'

CHAPTER THIRTY-FIVE

Once inside Connor told the judge to sit at the desk.

'I'll make a deal with you. Write out what I tell you, witness it and you can ride out of here and back to whatever sewer you came from.'

The judge wrote out the story of dealings of McLeish and Hawley, the hiring of outlaws to intimidate the inhabitants of Bernville and their part in falsely accusing Connor of wrongdoing.

'Now get the Hell out of my sight,' Connor ordered. 'I hope I never have to deal with a snake like you again. And if you ever try to cause trouble for me or the people of this town I'll expose you for the charlatan you are.'

No sooner had the frightened judge left than Connor collapsed across the desk.

That was how they found him when they came looking. With great care they placed the unconscious man on a stretcher and carried him to Doctor Lytton's surgery.

Doctor Lytton poked his head inside the room. Connor was propped up in bed reading his favourite book.

'Are you up to receiving a host of visitors?' he asked.

Connor raised his eyebrows and nodded but then shook his head.

'Hang on a moment; I'm tired of this invalid business. I'm getting up. Tell them to wait while I get dressed.'

'I'll put them in the parlour.'

Connor walked into the parlour and gazed around at his visitors. Alexander and Emma jumped to their feet and rushed to greet him. Smiling over at him and remaining seated were Jude and Catherine.

'It's good to see you on your feet again,' Jude remarked, after the children had ceased to fuss.

Doctor Lytton came in carrying a tray with cups and a pot of coffee. The doctor handed out sarsaparilla to the children and Catherine jumped up to serve the coffee. She also produced a bag of cookies, which she handed around.

'Well, what's been happening?' Connor asked.

'We've formed a trust for Emma and Alexander so the ranch will remain safely in their names. Catherine and me and Doc are trustees of the estate till they come of age.'

'That sounds like good sense.'

'We also applied to adopt the children but were turned down. The court ruled they could only go to a married couple. So Catherine and me ... I ... we want to get married so as we can look after them. We were hoping you would perform the wedding for us.'

A slow smile spread across Connor's face. He glanced at Catherine but she was looking down at her coffee and blushing furiously.

'Well, if that ain't the best news I've heard in a coon's age. Congratulations, I never performed a wedding afore but I am honoured to be asked. I never got to thank you for the help you rendered me when I was in jail, Catherine. It was a very brave thing to do. If you'd been caught those rogues would have thought nothing of shooting you. And as for you, Jude, if you hadn't cut loose with that rifle down the livery I'd be crow bait by now.'

It was a week later and the church was crowded to witness the wedding. Catherine's father proudly walked down the aisle thinking it was a marriage of convenience that amalgamated his own dry goods business with that of the livery and funeral parlour. Catherine was pleased to be getting married and leaving behind her spinsterhood. Jude was in a daze at his good fortune, having given up hope long ago of ever finding any woman willing to marry him. Alexander and Emma, the bride's attendants, looked flushed and happy in their new outfits.

The reception was a lavish affair held in the Golden Egg with plenty of good food and liquor. A slightly drunk Jude weaved a course over to sit beside Connor.

'Jason, this is the happiest day of my life,' he averred. 'And to think it would never have come about if you hadn't happened by.'

Connor smiled indulgently.

'I'm glad I was of some use.'

Jude cackled loudly.

'That's putting it mildly. Why don't you find yourself a good woman and get married and settle down?'

Connor shook his head.

'I don't think so. My wandering life would not suit a female.'

It took a moment for Connor's meaning to sink in.

'A wandering life – surely you are settled in Bernville with all your friends around you?'

'It is my fate, Jude, to wander the face of the earth. I am the instrument of God. Somewhere out there are folk, even now awaiting my help. I would be neglecting my mission in life to take things easy and settle down to town life. I must move on and do the Lord's work.

'Behold the days come, saith the Lord that I will send onto him a restlessness that causes him to wander and he shall empty their vessels and break their bottles.'